The GIRLS of the FIFTIES

Shirley E. Dodding

Edited by Elaine M. Baertl

The Girls of the Fifties

Tellwell Talent
www.tellwell.ca

ISBN
978-1-7-7962397-3 (Paperback)

To Joanne

Shirley Ellen Dodding

Enjoy!

ABOUT THE AUTHOR

Shirley Ellen Dodding is a retired Grade Seven Teacher, turned Novelist. She lives in the interior of British Columbia with her blended family.

Other books by Shirley Dodding:

You Look Just Like Her
Naked on the Inside
Dancing with the Stripes
Michael & Brie

Asparagus to Computers (non - fiction)

To Mom and Dad

ACKNOWLEDGMENTS

I would like to give a huge thank - you to Pam and Brian Evans, who sat on the beach in Penticton, two summers in a row, and gave invaluable comments and facts about living in the 1950's.

I also want to thank a social group, who walked and talked about living their lives in the 50's.

THIS NOVEL IS TWENTY - THREE YEARS LATE. STACEY IN THE NOVEL AND HER SISTER LEANNE, HAVE BEEN ON MY MIND ALL THAT TIME. THS IS A STORY OF LOVE, FRIENDSHIP, SISTERHOOD AND SUSPENSE DURING POST WORLD WAR II.

Chapter One

It was September, 1958. The trees were shimmering with daytime heat, every bough hanging low as if in shame. Later in the evening, with their heads lifted, they offered themselves to the world. The night was cooler and the trees sighed a huge relief.

This was the time of night Stacey loved the most, but her nine year old, young life, did not offer her the chance to be out late.

"Stacey you are not going out in the dark, you will not be doing anything outside, just because you feel like it. You will not sneak out either! I'm watching you and there will be no leniency if caught." As usual, mom was always right, even though she was over the top tough.

"But mom, there is no other way to get all the pop bottles everyone leaves behind on the road side or in the park. If I don't go now, everyone else will have money from bottles and I won't."

"First of all, who is everyone else, and second of all what do they, or you, need money for?" Mom's stern voice echoed anger.

Stacey did not want to tell her mom that for every cent she gleaned from cashing in bottles she put half into a savings and the other half she bought penny candy. Of course, if her mom knew she bought penny candy she would never let her go out. The dentist bill is threatening to tell all.

We lived in Surrey B.C. British Columbia, the furthest province west in Canada. Every spring with countless rains, the wide ditches along the roadside, would fill up with water, and the slow moving water would stink by June. I remember my cousin, tiny and not paying attention to anything, would play by the ditches, fall in, and before we knew it he was being dragged out by anyone in the neighbourhood who saw him first. We were lucky no one drowned. Little Keenan would not listen and his antics kept up all spring and summer until the heat from the sun, in the hottest part of July, declared the ditches dry. That was the only time anyone felt safe.

There was no letting up regarding the heat. The heat at the pool at the end of the street was lethal. Humidity was high, forcing every kid on the street to find cool shade.

Of course, if there were tree boughs dangling over the pool there would be shade. However, the pool in the park and the park itself were the bleakest areas in Surrey. Whoever designed the area, left no room for aesthetics. Young children ran home screaming with burns from the hottest sun on record one year; all it would have taken is a few planted trees and automated sprinklers to keep the kids cool.

I was one of those kids. I ran home screaming with burnt shoulders and coupled with getting a lecture from my mom, I received special ointment to ease the pain. From that day on, I always wore a cover over my shoulders, either a thin shirt, a towel, or on the worst days, I carried a sun umbrella.

The low, round wall of the pool was rough. Also, when walking into the pool, the uneven cement finishing, clawed at one's feet. There was no diving, or swimming laps, the water was only up to the middle of the thighs of most kids. Of course, it depended on the age of the kids or how tall they were.

At times, the water looked green and wading into it felt like wading into a slough. This did not stop any of the neighbourhood kids. The cool effect of the water was the opposite to the hard cement floor, and the relentless sun.

The wall of the pool was so low it felt as though all the water was going to splash out any minute. When older kids ran in and around the circumference, the swooshing water splashed all over the ground. The cement floor inside the pool, was seen once again, rough and bleak.

I cannot remember if there was a lifeguard. Our Mom was a great swimmer, and could have applied if they needed one. She passed her swimming test, but not the written test. I sure wish she had because there were times when it looked as though she felt sad about it. It also would have given her a little cash. Instead, she found a great way to make ends meet, which was one of her favourite sayings, 'to make ends meet.'

She found a way to make extra money, working in the garden at her Mom and Dad's. This gave her freedom and a reason to get away from the house, once a week. They were my grandparents, whom Leanne and I thought were so cute. They were short, little and grandma walked bent over.

I still remember visiting them on weekends. My Grandpa grew beans so tall, I could not find my sister in them. My Mom would go there every Tuesday to do Grandma's hair and in return, we would walk away with our arms full of chard, turnips, lettuce, carrots and of course beans. It wasn't until I was older, I realized this helped our food budget by a large amount. Produce was expensive, but my Mom unbeknown to my sister and I set up a trade. Grandma's hair done every week for arms full of vegetables. She was clever in that respect.

Food was a big draw at the time. My sister and I would be skipping on the sidewalk and Mom would be shelling peas on the front porch. She enjoyed being a housewife, those days in the fifties. Life was simple.

When our Dad arrived home everything would stop in preparation for dinner. My sister, and I would be requisitioned to set the table, while mom had steaming pots of potatoes, carrots, and turnips cooking on the stove. It has been noted by others that the vegetables would be cooked to death in those years.

Before that, we would be sent early to the root cellar, which was a designated area in the back yard. There, we would gather potatoes and carrots, and on the way through the back corridor we would visit the pantry shelves for a quart of canned peaches or apricots, whichever our mom chose for the meal that night. Even on hot summer days mom was always canning.

Of course, there would be shopping for the meat at a butchers earlier that day, fresh meat bought and wrapped in newspaper. The meat for dinner (being cooked in the oven) was the most important to working men, (I could sense this without being told). It was not only the most prized item at dinner, but the most expensive.

My Dad called it a joint. Whenever he visited the grandparents he would go in loud and brash with one question. Do you have your joint in the oven, ma?

While the women of the house would be preparing dinner Dad would be in his favourite large recliner, with his feet up, a Stogie in his mouth, or on other days, a pipe jammed to the brim with tobacco. He would have slippers on his feet, but whoa to him if he sat in the front room with his work clothes on. He did respect Mom's wishes, even though there were times when she wanted things done her way, a little too fast.

This was apparent on the days, when a neighbour came over, and Dad had not changed yet. Dad was a mason and quite often he would come home with mortar in his pant cuffs.

He would entertain his visitors in the front room, and all her wishes about changing his clothes were out the window. He was always happy to see people. It took him away from the ordinary. Leanne and I knew however, there would be words at the dinner table.

We as kids, learned to gauge the weather, or some would say the downright climate in the house at any given hour. On nights where Dad refused to be led around by the nose, we established a time to disappear into our bedroom. The disappearing act occurred when the dessert came out, and we would carry our jello or chiffon cake into our bedroom. We could hear the mumbling, not fighting yet, but words being said.

Our house was small. We had to walk across a huge flat, floor vent between two end walls, to get to our bedroom. This vent was pitch black, the size of a double couch. It looked like an immense grate with large holes in it. When the air from the furnace came on, the whoosh of it, scared both of us, all the time. When we were trying to get across the massive floor vent to get to our bedroom, and if we had a skirt on, (in those days we wore skirts to school, no pants allowed), our skirts would be whipped up, flying around our waist.

Leanne and I shared a bedroom, so it was easy to talk and have someone to complain to or to celebrate with, on special occasions. I still remember eating chiffon cake with icing, or upside down cake dripping with peaches or raspberries. To this day my sister loves chiffon cake. If I gave her that for her birthday, I would not have to buy her a present.

In the fifties, there were many food choices. A homemaker, like our Mother, would almost memorize the recipes from Jean Pare's cookbooks. She had books on appetizers: shrimp cocktail, cucumber canapés, main courses: Salisbury steak, beef stroganoff, casseroles, and meat loaf. My favourite was the meal with Yorkshire Puddings. The house would smell of hot grease fat, the minute I arrived home from school. I would jump for joy as I knew what we were having for dinner that night.

Some of the other favourites were dessert dishes. My overall fancy favourite, was Baked Alaska. I asked a waiter in a restaurant once, when I was older, how to make that and he explained it well. I looked back thinking; how did our Mom do that?

Chapter Two

My sister, was taller than I. She had longer legs, and a longer neck. Her countenance was soft and gentle. I don't think I have ever heard her swear. She was, our Mom would brag, fourteen months older than myself. She would say, now Stacey, you mind your older sister. She would go down the block to visit a relative, but be back before I would have time to tell my sister off. I loved her, but she would not move on anything. She would not take a risk. I wanted her to come out with me after dark and pick bottles, but she wouldn't. "Mom said no."

"Ok then, let's go when it's really dark and Mom won't know." She wouldn't.

There were times when I would have liked to have strangled my sister. She, in turn, would have liked to walk away from me, many times. I remember her saying at one time, that she thought I was on a plateau, or higher up platform, the way I acted. We argued constantly, about everything. Our Mom would say, "Now, you girls get along."

"Yah, I would have liked to get along ... without her, and walk away anytime. But, of course mom's voice was prominent in my head." My sister, I knew felt the same way at times.

My sister, would watch everything and then draw a conclusion. She came up with answers and reasons I would never have dreamed of. When I think about how different she was, and how differently she looked at life, I knew something must have been up.

I asked my mom one day if she was my real sister or if she was adopted. Mom pointed to her stomach and said she made my sister in there.

I said, *I'm not so sure*, in my head of course. There is no being cheeky to the Mom of the house.

When we were bored we would go down the street to visit our cousin Bernadette. One block away and yet so far.

Bernadette was the only girl in a family of six kids. She had five brothers and she was a lot busier than Leanne and I on any given day. She helped with the cooking, the laundry and the disciplining of the youngest. One of these younger boys was Keenan, you know, the one who always fell into ditches. When the neighbours pulled him out, it was nothing but work for Bernadette.

She had to wash his hair and change his clothes all over again. Bernadette ran the house, the mother was no longer there. Nobody knew where she went. Luckily, the father had a good paying job and was able to feed the clan.

I swore on a stack of bibles one day, Bernadette was going to blow a gasket, but she had a sense of humour that would knock your socks off. Everything had humour to it, and her laugh could be heard in the house, to anyone outside hanging up clothes, and then it could be heard all the way down the street, when Leanne and I were walking home.

Bernadette, not only had skills beyond her sixteen years, but she had the most beautiful hair I had ever seen. She was a brunette. Her long shiny curls gently folded themselves down her back and down her chest. I could see how they named her Bernadette, because it sounded so close to brunette, the colour of her hair.

There was no lack of suitors for her. My Mom would use the word suitors, and I would envision a bunch of guys lined up at her door wearing suits. Bernadette was not interested in suitors. She was more interested in making sure her younger brothers ate well, had good lunches and did well in school. More than that, she was happiest when they at least stayed in school. She was adamant she would not have a bunch of rough, unclean boys around, who were dumb. She used the work dumb a lot, then she would laugh!

One day when Keenan fell into the ditch twice, she was done. Ok, then you will sit in that muck until dad gets home. That made all the boys sit up and listen.

Her dad came home and there was a lot of yelling, then a lot of strapping. Keenan did not fall into, or go close to the ditches again, rain water filled, or dry.

I lost track of our cousin Bernadette a few years later. She fell in love with one of her suitors and left the clan. Her dad remarried, but I never did know what happened to all the boys. I think Bernadette sees the youngest now and again. She ended up on a ranch.

The next summer was even hotter than the last. The yelps from the park could be heard all the way down the street. It appeared as though every neighbourhood kid was at the park, running through the water then laying on the skimpy grass, always soaking wet with the sloshed water spilling out of the pool.

Leanne and I were walking down our street one day, only half way this time. Our friend Mary - Jane lived there, and we were picking her up to go to the park. She was ten, and an only child. Her mom and dad were from Holland. Another word for Holland, I found out later was

The Netherlands. Mary - Jane was tall and slim, with blue eyes and blond hair which her mom curled in rags. Mrs. Hoek was an older mother; I swear she was fifty when she had Mary - Jane.

Walking into their front room, which then extended further back into a kitchen, was different for me. I remember seeing crisp, white doilies and furniture polished to such a gleam, it hurt my eyes.

Mrs. Hoek was standing at the sink in the semi dark kitchen scraping the skin off the carrots. I was always amazed at how she did things. In the sink was a triangular shaped, green jelly like container, with holes in it. Water would run through the holes, but the container held all the scraps from the vegetables, Mrs. Hoek pealed. She had a garden in the back which covered half of the back yard. The rest was a huge lawn which Mr. Hoek mowed every week.

When she finished peeling everything for the evening meal, she would take the green jelly like container to the garden, and dump it, where all the other scraps were. She called this her compost. In actuality it became the fertilizer for her garden only after many months of rotting. My sister and I found this extremely interesting. Mostly my sister, however, as she always did love plants and plant growth. When we were leaving to go to the park, Mary - Jane kissed her mother good-bye, on the cheek. I also found this different. It must have been different in Holland. Girls were sure to respect their Mothers, and not feel scorned by them. Don't get me wrong, I loved my Mother, but I didn't kiss her every time I went to the pool. Mr. Hoek came into the house just then. Yikes, he was even older than Mrs. Hoek! Then, I started wondering, was Mary - Jane adopted? I asked her once; she said no.

Mr. Hoek would come out onto the front porch each night we walked there, to pick up Mary - Jane. He always watched us, like he was wise and willing to share it, but nobody ended up talking to him. I never did know where he worked. His name was Claude.

Mrs. Hoek, at times, would come out onto the front porch in the morning and blow her nose. I always wondered why she would do that on the front porch, with numerous neighbours going about their daily chores. She would watch all the neighbourhood kids go to school. I still didn't know much about her, except her first name was Helen.

The school was at the opposite end of the street from the pool. When all the kids were off the street and in the school yard, only then would Mrs. Hoek go back inside the house. I only knew this because others who saw her would mention it and wonder why as well.

In the summer time, all the neighbourhood kids would put on skits and perform them for the adults on the huge lawn at the back of Mary - Jane's house. Mr. Hoek was proud we would use his space, so he kept it nibble clean, the lawn so perfectly mowed it was as though he hired goats to chew it evenly.

Our plays were good. I was the Master of Ceremonies and introduced each player as though we were a Shakespearean troupe. All the parents were lined up on chairs in rows, as if in a theatre, but first they had to pay twenty - five cents to get in.

I'm not sure who I entrusted the money too. We always had enough to buy treats after the show, especially on the hottest of days. Leanne knew a better way. She wanted our money to be offered to the needy. We put our money out there and the radio station put our names on the radio as a group of young neighbourhood actors who helped others. When all of our names were being announced on the radio, one by one; we all whooped for joy.

Unbeknown to most of the neighbourhood kids, I noticed a man next door to where Claude Hoek kept his lawn mower and supplies. When I stood in front of the parents to introduce our next play, I could see him out of the corner of my eye. His property was adjacent to the back yard play area, but he always watched us behind a pole or a bush. The parents could not see him, but I could. One day, I will tell Leanne, although, I don't want to scare her.

Chapter Three

One day, I asked Claude Hoek a question. He was extremely shy, but very forthright and explicit. I asked him about his neighbour at the back of his house. He replied, by telling me the reclusive man whom I must have seen was Mr. Felix Wolk. Mr. Wolk had a tragic childhood and even a more tragic teenage era leading up to now. Claude Hoek refused to say too much more. As it was, I was interested in how he knew that much about him anyway.

Once again, I chose to find out my own way and not ask too many questions. I chose not to tell Leanne yet, as she would worry and not feel comfortable going into the back yard again. Like I said she does not take risks. I however, was keen to know as much as I could. The safety of the cast in our plays, I was sure was at stake. I felt responsible somehow, being the MC and all.

School in the fifties was strict, straight laced and at times scary. The teachers were stern, not a lot of laughter there. I do remember Bernadette however, bless her heart, making some teachers laugh. She was an enigma... whatever, that means.

I loved school. I wrote my name Stacey on all my books, my lunch kit, my pencils, my boots, shoes and even my umbrella. Woe is me if I lost anything and had to buy another. My Mother was adamant about that. I even wrote my last name, which was Sullivan on everything, where it would fit. We were the Sullivan sisters.

The only thing I didn't like about school was they used the strap on unruly students...mostly boys. I have to admit I don't remember any girls putting their palms flat out to feel the strong sting of the leather strap, raised high, then low. The hurt was not only the physical hurt, but the emotional hurt as well. I think shortly after that, the strap was abandoned.

School had opportunities for singing, drama, athletic teams and cheerleader squads. I watched the cheerleader squad and decided when I was older I would join.

My sister joined a club that was quiet like her. It was a spelling study group for grade fives. She found some good friends in it, who did not judge her regarding her unique way of looking at things. My sister turned out to be a good speller, so I was not sure why she joined that group. I think she needed the positives in her life more than I did. She felt, I thought, overwhelmed at times, at home. Mom was not one for giving out praises and Dad was at times more negative than positive. Me, I just did not care enough. I just went my own way.

I remember, one crazy class game we played. We had to write down something about each other, on their own sheet, when we were sitting in a circle.

I remember someone writing on my sheet, that I didn't seem to like people. I would never do that to a class because I remember that little horrible, written note, which was not true. I loved people, I just didn't like myself. I didn't like myself because my face was full of pimples and I would not even look in a mirror. I was always at war with my face.

My sister made some great friends, to this day she still has those same friends. The girls of the fifties were kind, loyal and true. They never gave each other up for anything, loyal to the end.

As we all got older we wore the poodle skirts, the bobby socks, and the white and black oxfords. Music in the fifties, was the best. Whenever, the blues came on, we would dance with each other, even putting our cheek on each other's shoulder, as if mooning over a boy.

At the sock hops, which were dances at lunchtime, the gym floor would be full of girls in their long, wide skirts, tight sweaters, long pony tails, satin neck scarves (tied with one knot and turned sideways) and pink lipstick.

If a boy asked one of us to dance, the others were so jealous they just looked away, until someone asked them. The boys wore dazzling white T – shirts (like they were scrubbed on a rock), blue jeans and black leather jackets. Their hair was long on the side and on the top, but slicked down to be almost greasy looking.

After school we would all go home, complete our homework, then as a group, we would have the freedom to take off and go up into the hills, as long as we were home by dinner.

At night we would play Kick the Can. It had to be dark to play this game, as nobody was supposed to see the person kicking the can. Once the can was kicked, the kicker could grab as many 'opposite' team players as time permitted, to put them into a pretend jail. If the other team kicked the can next they could free all the players held in the jail. "We won!" could be heard all over the neighbourhood.

The next game would be Red Rover. All the kids would throw their arms around each other's shoulders and connect like a long string. There would be two teams. The caller would invite someone from the opposing side to come over. The object of the game was to NOT let any runner crash through the linked arms.

The team inviting the person over would try to invite the weakest person. This way the weakest person could not get through the strong armed hold, on the string line. If they did not get through they had to link onto the end of the string line to make that team larger, and hopefully stronger.

"Red Rover, Red Rover I invite Stacey over." If they invited me it was at the end of the game. I thought I was tough, so I would barrel through their arms and break up the whole chain.

All I could hear was, "Ya, just kill us all." They were mad that I was stronger than they thought. The guys were brutal in this game.

At the end of the game, if it ended like that, everyone went home. There was no use complaining or getting mad at each other, we were all friends, and it was just a game.

Another game we played was Capture the Flag. Again, there were two opposing teams. The coloured flag would be pushed into the ground in an open area. Each team member tried to sneak up to grab the flag, hopefully, without being caught by an opposing team member. If caught, they were put into a pretend jail. Once the flag was grabbed, the person ran as fast as they could across their own line. When the flag was captured the whole team carried the winning team member on their shoulders. There was a lot of noise in this game.

When we went home almost every kid would have homemade bread from the bread box smothered with butter, or a piece of homemade cake cut from the cake on a cake stand. This cake stand, to me, always looked like a huge wine glass with a long glass stem.

On weekends, we would play double Dutch, or marbles, hopscotch or yo yo's. The guys loved the marbles. Winning a tiger's eye would be the most prestigious award and the younger boys would sit for hours on the cold cement with their legs apart trying to win the most valuable marble in their eyes, for their collection.

Leanne and I played Double Dutch together. We had songs we would sing, but right now I can't think of one. Girls would line up and try to get into the two overlapping ropes without stopping them. If they won a count more than what the last skipper had, we would all stand over them after, clapping our hands like the song, The Cheese Stands Still.

"You can't just stand there, you have to jump in!" This was the chant of all the girls when one girl on the side lines took too long. One girl Elma, was scared, and it wasn't until the end of the skipping season before she actually cleared the jump into the two over-lapping ropes. In the end she probably had the most skipping counts.

School days were over, and my family loved it; they were campers. Leanne and I helped Mom pack food and clothing (for hot days and for rainy days). Mom was always ready for anything. Of course, we packed enough insect repellent to drown a beehive and enough sun tan lotion and burn lotion to rival Walmart. We were camping once again at Shuswap Lake in the interior of B.C. We never knew who we would meet there, or what adventure awaited us.

Part Two

Chapter Four

We were given our report cards, a ticket for the P.N.E. and sent on home. The school year was over. Everyone within hearing distance yelled: NO MORE PENCILS, NO MORE BOOKS, NO MORE TEACHER'S DIRTY LOOKS.

It was time to go camping. No sooner did we get home, we were packing our green car with everything we would need. I remember, even as a nine year old, the pride my Dad took in his car. It was square and large. He said it was a 1956 Buick. For some reason, I remembered that well.

Shuswap Lake was in the interior of British Columbia. From where we lived in Surrey, on the coast, this popular camping spot was almost six hours away. It may have been less other years, but this year there was construction on the road. Many stops were endured in the hot sun, luckily, we had coolers full of food and drinks; thanks once again, to our Mom's perfect planning. The only thing that did not do well were the brownies. They ended up being a blob of chocolate on wax paper, especially when the ice cubes in the cooler started to melt.

The road construction was slow, and even after three weeks, when we drove home, there was the inevitable wait. My Dad would be so impatient, there was a lot of swearing, and to this day I don't know how many Stogies he went through. Between those, and the pipe packed with tobacco to the rim, the car was an incinerator.

When we finally arrived, at the entrance to the campsite, it was a major relief. I remember the large chiseled expanse of wood at the front entrance with the logo introducing Shuswap Lakes. The camp-ground had over 250 sites. We were hoping for one close to the lake. Every site had huge trees taking a gracious bough with numerous green branches. I think some were cedar, some were coniferous, green all year.

There were also deciduous trees which changed colours in the fall, just when we were leaving to go back to school. With a bit of flirtatious wind, the leaves would turn inside out. I loved the way the leaves turned over and then back again, showing the underside. Then the whole top of the tree would be caught by a strong wind and be whooshed to one side. The branches would co-operate dropping the leaves onto the ground, displaying a carpet of colour.

The flirtation of the leaves gave the feeling of freedom. Freedom untangled. I loved the idea of being outside and not having to be in a routine, or hear Mom say, "No, you're not going out to pick bottles, it's getting dark."

It was almost dark when we arrived that night. The trip had taken its toll on all of us. Dad, tired from driving, Mom tired from guarding the cooler, my sister and I from fighting over comic books or whatever else we brought, thinking we would be entertained.

Now that we were parked in a campsite, there was Mom again giving orders. "OK, now you girls drag all the gear out of the trunk, then take the pails and go and get water at the outside tap down the lane. Then when you get back help your father put up the tent." She sashayed over to the picnic table.

I felt like saying, "What are you going to do Mom?" I however, was not brought up like that, so of course I kept my big mouth shut. She, however, had the most important job of all – she was setting up to make dinner. Her first move was to get the Coleman camp stove onto the end of the picnic table. This was not just a half hazard type of job. This job had a lot of merit.

First of all the green camp stove had to be on the end of the picnic table, whereby, anyone standing over it cooking would have to face the lane where traffic drove by. Our Mom always needed to see what was happening and not have her back to anything. I always thought this was like a Mother bear with her cubs. It felt secure and safe for us.

When Leanne and I returned with the sploshing buckets of water, we were always given a mind about how much we wasted. We however, could not help it, because man, that water was heavy.

When we finished with the water pails we helped Dad resurrect the tent. The steel poles had be fitted together in the middle and tight on the corners. Over time, the poles became difficult to link together so Dad had to really push hard to attach them. Once a square was made with the four poles, then laid on the ground, Dad would go under the front flap and stand in the middle. He would join two, larger poles together, then push the long rod up to make a pointed roof. With a screw driver the two larger rods would be tightened in the middle.

A camping nightmare would be, if the middle pole collapsed in the night, or when there was a storm. All four of us would have the tent on our faces.

After the tent was up it was my job, along with Leanne, to load all the sleeping bags, pillows, soft suitcases, and duffel bags into the interior of the tent and set it up the way we always do. Dad, always slept close to the opening. That made us all feel protected.

Once we were finished with all of this work, we were starving. Mom had a flowered, oil table cloth on the scrubbed down picnic table. All the plates and utensils were lined up with a lovely tiny vase of wild flowers in the middle; these she must have picked unbeknown to us, while we were working on the tent. She must have scoured the road side because where I was standing, I could see no yellow or purple flowers.

We had steak, cooked to perfection, and potatoes in foil with cut up green onions and sour cream. There were carrots and turnips, (not my favourite), but also a green salad. Of course for dessert there was the ever present chiffon cake. We rarely saw jello at the campsite or brownies. They became a liquid mess and when we were close, we could hear our Mom swear. She never swore.

Dad loved the dinner that first night. It was almost as though he looked forward to it all day, after the stress of driving to the campsite.

After dinner, I can still see and hear Dad chop, chop, chopping wood for the next hour, so we could have a great campfire every night. My sister and I were forever doing dishes when Dad chopped wood. I would wash and Leanne would dry, then the next night we would switch. We would slap each other on the thigh with a semi wet tea towel, then we would run away to not become hit again. Mom would get so mad at us, because the sudsy, hot water would be cold just when we had to wash a sticky frying pan.

It took awhile to heat the water for the dishes so this became a thorn in her side. While we were previously eating dinner, the hot water was being heated on the Coleman stove for washing dishes. We learned the hard way, to not slap each other with damp tea towels. We needed to use the hot water first, to finish the dishes, then we would take our war to the lake.

So after dinner, it was well known this was Mom's alone time. She would wander down to the washroom, or take a stroll down the lane. One thing she loved to do was to look for a wide, green, fallen branch which was thrust to the ground, in a wind storm. The branch was large with a lot of needles. It had to have a wooden end to serve as a handle. This would be her broom. She would move dirt and pebbles from around the tent and from around the picnic table to make everything look swept, neat and tidy. After a few days all the items in the tent would be stacked in one corner. The area we walked into every day would also be swept out.

Her methods of improvising were adorable. We were content with substitutions. A large, green tree branch, for a broom, a swirl of bark for a vase, wildflowers for store bought flowers and a list of others as the camping days moved along.

Dad was happy with being outside so much, he rarely wanted to go home. His time outside meant he could be in his favourite, five horse power boat and fish all day. The quiet was like a sauna to his soul. Mom was not in a demanding mood, so Dad was left alone to be his own man.

Quite often Dad was out in his small skiff alone. We could see his camping hat, complete with fly fish all around the brim. He had his fly fishing rod in the lake and a Stogie in his mouth. His face was relaxed and when he looked up, we waved to him from the beach. He was smart, he always wore a bright red life jacket. He couldn't swim.

The days he caught fish were the best. Leanne and I could see how proud he felt, like a real hunter going out to kill for his family. The most exciting day of all was when Leanne caught a fish. I think it was eight pounds. She held it up in front of her on a threadlike fishing line with the sun beaming behind her. We all praised her and Mom took a picture with her box camera. The fish looked large in front of her young, slim body.

Dad taught us how to gut a fish. The sharp knife slit down the middle, the guts pulled out, but the long, fragile skeleton had to be picked up and pulled out in one piece, first. If this spine was taken out without care, there would be small bones in the fish when cooked. There was always a comment from Mom.

"You girls be careful you don't choke on the small bones," Mom would be adamant she was not going to be happy, if she had to nurse anyone, choking to death.

The smell of fresh fish, fried in butter, in a searing hot frying pan cooked over a Coleman stove, outside camping, was the best smell ever.

For some reason I cannot remember what we ate with that delicious fish. It may have been Mom's potato salad. This was a main stay in those days, especially in the summer.

Whenever, Mom and Dad had people over or went to a party, Mom was always asked to bring her potato salad. She used hard boiled eggs in it as well as potatoes, celery and spices. It did taste good paired with the buttery fish. There was always a green salad as well, thankful once again for Grandpa's garden of vegetables.

After dinner there was time for cookies, cake, fruit or any of the candies we used to eat. There was such a choice: jaw breakers, chicken bones, (small, crunchy, sugary, and bone shaped), licorice pipes, tiny marshmallow bananas, bolo balls and of course the ever present double bubble gum.

The double bubble gum was such a great treat at the end of the day. We would walk down the lane, unwrap the little square white package, take out the bright pink gum, and then unfold the comic strip which was around the gum.

I remember the pink gum had a definite line down the middle. It looked like it was meant to be broken in half to share with someone else. I also remember, my sister sharing half of her gum with me at times. I probably dropped mine in the dirt more than she did.

As we chewed the gum which was a little hard at first, we would be reading the comic strip, then we would trade it with whoever was with us at the time. As we passed the comic strip around, the gum in our mouths was becoming softer, and then the competition for blowing the biggest bubble would begin.

By this time, Mom would be glad for us to be gone, so we stayed away. We would walk the lanes blowing and popping bubbles for the next hour or so. The campsite lanes at the Shuswap were all named after fish, so anyone interested in fish were offered up names that were easy to pronounce, like Coho, or harder, like Dolly Varden. Dad always talked about the Dolly Varden. He thought they tasted the best.

We were only allowed to stay out until it looked and felt darker. We were able to gauge the time by the trees and the sun hidden behind them. Once we arrived back at the campsite we were asked to find our hoodies in the tent, and sit around the campfire.

Dad had been working the whole time we were gone on splitting wood to make kindling. Those long thin sticks of wood, coupled with newspaper brought from home, would ignite the fire, and then smaller logs would be thrown on. I remember the sparks, which always stirred up and tore into the air, always with a sudden flurry.

Once the fire was a bright, electric yellow and burning steadily, other logs would be thrown on. Once the darkness hemmed us in, the largest of all the logs would be strategically placed. These logs would not be thrown on, they were heavy, and would have eroded the whole fire. They would take us through the night with a large fire base, complete with tall, licking flames. We would sing, make smores, sing and make more smores.

Our fingers were always sticky with smores, and the saplings we used for sticks to roast the marshmallows were just as sticky. The graham wafers top and bottom became soft with the melted chocolate, and a large roasted marshmallow jammed in the middle. This was an experience every camper, and every kid should have. We just had to be careful to not burn our mouths or tongues. Some kids liked to lick the stick.

Lights out meant we were in bed when it was pitch black and Leanne and I would talk endlessly, in the tent. Mom and dad would talk on the outside of the tent around the campfire. I never knew what they talked about but it was not arguing and fighting, like at home. Like I said, Dad was super happy outside, camping and not being told what to do.

That night there was a storm. "Oh, brother, we just got here and now it's raining." Leanne was so disappointed.

We were all lamenting the same thing. Mom popped into action of course, and ran around the outside of the tent putting all the flaps down. We had a long piece of canvas at the front entrance of the tent that could be pulled out about the length of a three seater couch and when tied to the ground on the front corners, it gave us a cover. We could stand under it and watch the rain fall.

The other flaps kept the upper tent canvas covered, so there was a second thickness on the top half. The water rolled down to the bottom half but there were no top leaks. I loved how this tent was made. I was trying to see the people who made it, in my mind, in some small impoverished country, I was sure.

While Leanne and Mom protected the tent, Dad and I moved the cut wood as fast as we could. If the wood was wet, so were we. Being wet at a campsite was the worst, there was no place to get dry and warm again, unless the sun beat down on us the next day. If the wood was wet, the chance of a warm fire that night was limited.

My sister and I were now inside the tent. Mom and Dad were wearing their slickers - rubber type yellow jackets, pants and goofy hats with ear flaps, but they were kept dry. They chose to stay out to make sure nothing would blow away. The campfire had undisciplined embers, so the dark was held at bay.

It was such a great feeling, being inside the tent all warm and cozy. We were however, starting to get a little bored so we were play fighting, trying to push each other off the buckled up sleeping bags.

We were both pushed off balance and shoulder nudged the side of the tent which was unbeknown to us, saturated with water. The only problem was, we had no idea what was happening on the outside of the tent. As our bodies on the inside nudged the canvas, the outside was leaking water. After awhile the water leaked through the canvas and was sitting at our feet right inside the tent.

``Oh, no, we`re in trouble now!`` No sooner had we both realized this when in came Mom, and boy was she mad! It took us an hour, soaking up water with towels, to make the inside of the tent dry again. We girls were scorned and told to move all the bedding into the middle of the tent. We were now all sleeping like sausages in the driest area of the tent.

I could see Dad smiling while he puffed on his pipe. I knew what he was thinking. He thought any juvenile mishap, was more fun, than pure boredom. We were all a little cold that night.

Of course, the next day was no fun for Leanne and I. We were being punished by dragging out every sheet, blanket, and sleeping bag to put over clothes lines to dry out, with hope it did not rain again.

The day was a brilliant gold. The sun shone so bright, by noon all the clothesline items were dry. We now had to roll them all up and put them back into the tent.

After that, we had lunch and then we were free until dinner. This was the best part of the trip, when we were free to wander the camp site, see and discover new things.

One curiosity for me, was a campsite we had passed, when we were blowing bubbles the night before. The campsite had a family of four in it, two of the four were girls about our age. They looked interesting to me, but somehow not from our city or country. I had a feeling about this, so was hoping there would be a chance to talk to them.

We lingered around the water tap across from their campsite. I remember them looking at us. Leanne noted they were staring at us because we were literally staring at them.

"Come on, let's go," she said. "We can't just stare at them." Leanne was right, so we moved on. I was adamant that the next night we would make a connection, and for sure, introduce ourselves.

I was always interested in other countries. I spent time pouring over maps and riveted to the countries in Europe. It seemed to me it would be so romantic to visit Paris, or some other city that had a totally different culture than we did in Canada. I could envision myself sitting at a tiny, circular table outside, on a strip of cobblestones, in Paris, drinking from a sophisticated glass. Of course, this would be when I was older. I was only nine, but I had these visions which were so much fun to fabricate.

The next day we passed by the campsite again. This time, the two girls were at the water tap. They lifted their heads and gave us their most welcome smiles.

As we walked by, we smiled back and said hello. They also said hello, but it certainly was not a hello like ours. We could tell it was a greeting by their body language, but not for sure if it was a hello.

I loved how they looked. One girl had dark hair, the other one had hair which was lighter. The most interesting point however, was what they were wearing. I think it was pantaloons. Those loose fitting pants were tight around the waist and ankles, but billowed down the leg.

They were navy blue. I did not know the tops they were wearing, but the billowing pants, I distinctly remember.

A couple of days went by before we saw them again. This time I was certain we were going to connect in a conversation.

Leanne was chatty at the campsite that night. "Stacey was obsessed with these girls. It was all she could talk about. She was so sure they were from a city in Europe. She just could not figure it out at the time." Leanne went on to say she was sure there would be a meeting time, where all four would be able to share something.

"When the time arrived it was as though we knew these girls all our lives. They were from a city in Europe just as Stacey predicted. They were from Amsterdam. This was a city in Holland, or some would say the Netherlands. These girls would be like Mary - Jane on our street in Surrey. Mr. and Mrs. Hoek would have loved to talk to them, including the parents. What a coincidence they were all from Holland."

"When they spoke it was like a music box. The words went up and down as though on a musical ride. I loved to hear them talk." For once, it was great to hear someone else talk, not just me. I was telling Mom and Dad this. Stacey could not stress how excited she felt.

The names of the girls were Elle, and Evi. Even their names sounded musical to me. When we asked them questions about their home, country and school they were always so polite and answered in such a way, that could only have been taught.

Unfortunately, these girls were leaving the next day, but we were able to spend the whole afternoon and the early part of the evening with them.

They showed us what they do in Holland at recess and at lunch. In their hands they had two sticks. In between the sticks they had wool. The idea was to create a spider like web around the middle hole of the sticks by moving the sticks like knitting needles.

Once the inside was bare and the spider web around it was complete the game began. I knew it would take me longer than two days to learn it, so I just watched.

Elle and Evi used an assortment of colours. They not only made spider webs, but they made symmetrical spider webs with different colours of wool. The design was always symmetrical on both sides. This was a new word which I had learned in grade four math.

When they left the next morning, I wanted to get their address. They grinned at me because they really did live in Holland. How was I supposed to get there? Of course, I could have written.

They flew to Canada and rented equipment to camp. I thought wow, what a great way to see the country! I never did see or hear from them again. This encounter only made me realize how memories are so special. The memories of how these two were so polite and so caring I will never forget. I remember their pantaloons as well, navy blue and always the same.

Chapter Five

Back home, it was school again. Of course, we were outfitted with new underwear: T – shirts and under pants. Mom had a credit card for Eatons. We were allowed one pair of shoes. A few new tops and skirts, but our winter coats, come winter, would have to do, so off we went back to school.

I remember how we barely had enough money to buy school supplies, but we always made it through. I still think Mom had a little mason jar she kept hidden with an unprecedented amount of money for a rainy day.

Lucky for us, we were always dry, clean and warm. The food offered to us at home was fantastic. Even though we were not thrilled with deer, moose or elk meat we always had a freezer full and did not go hungry. Dad made sure of that.

In school, my sister Leanne and I helped with the food shelter. We helped pack food into little Styrofoam containers for students, who needed a hand out, especially at lunchtime.

I often wondered what they ate when they went home. I was more than happy to help. One day a little girl, either from kindergarten or grade one, sidled up by me and put her hand into mine. I felt this chill run over my whole body. I was so taken with this little child, I felt I knew my calling right there. I wanted to be a teacher.

Throughout the first six months Leanne and I helped serve the younger children at lunch. The little girl who put her hand into my hand continued to come to the soup shelter and she always came down my food line. Her little smile made my day not small, not medium, but enormous.

Once, when her teacher happened to be in the room, she noticed her student shining up to me. That's when she got the idea. The teacher, Mrs. Ferguson was at that time needing someone in the school to read stories to her class under her supervision of course. She mentioned she was looking in the older grades, but when she saw how Felicia was looking up to me, she thought she would ask.

I was so excited about the idea, I almost slopped soup all over the lovely paper table cloth, when I served that day.

Felica, did a little skip to her table and I was hooked.

"Wow, you really want me to read to the students?`

``I would like that very much.`` Mrs. Ferguson was sure of it.

She also mentioned a couple of things. She needed my Mom or Dad to sign a paper saying I was allowed to miss silent reading in my class at least twice a week. She also needed to confirm with the teacher I had that year, to see if I was able to escape my classroom, without it jeopardizing my own learning.

I followed Mrs. Ferguson to her classroom. She was a long way down another hall that I confess, I had not seen before.

``There are about one hundred books on the shelves in the classroom. I teach by theme, so all that needs to be done is to choose a book that matches the theme. Quite often the books are already pulled and standing up in the theme corner over here." She walked to a lovely corner that had the word September In large letters and all the items for the month. There were pictures of school kids, with back packs, lunch kits and in the corner there were classroom games.

The shelves below the counters were stuffed with books. I could see I would need some time to choose a book. I was allowed in at lunch to eat my lunch with the students and then look for the first book I would read to the class, every second day at 11:30. Of course, I had to make sure the book was long enough for the half hour. If not, I would be sure to choose two.

Mrs. Ferguson mentioned she had an errand to run so I went back to my own classroom, just in time for lunch to be over.

I took the papers to my parents and they were thrilled. They knew how much I loved books and loved to read. Leanne was happy for me as well. She had her own interests and her own friends to keep her busy and happy, so she did not depend on me to fill in her free times at school. Many of the girls skipped throughout the lunch time but two days a week I was going to spend in the grade one class reading books to them.

I was able to get to know Felicia. When I saw what she wore each day I realized she was from another country. Her clothing was simple but beautifully made. It took a couple of weeks before I learned she was from Mexico. Her little smile and long, dark hair made me think of what it would be like to live and work in Mexico.

Early in the fall, I was able to catch a glimpse of her parents. During an interview time they were sitting in the hall waiting to meet Mrs. Ferguson. They were happy looking and both were wearing once again, incredible clothing. I found out later they were all handmade.

Felicia, was doing well in school. She knew all her letters and sounds; her parents were so proud of her. I was walking down the hallway, just when their interview was over. Mrs. Ferguson stopped me and introduced me to the family. They were so overjoyed they both gave me a hug. ``Òur Felicia just loves you,`` they both said together. ``She loves you reading to her and to the whole class. Felicia is very affectionate and when she holds your hand she is showing great confidence in herself as she is growing up fast in Canada.``

As the days in school marched into late fall, all the leaves changed colour and the school ground was a carpet of red, yellow and orange. The whole school was electric with the change in weather and upcoming Hallowe`en. My books were just that, all fall and all about witches, cauldrons, candy and spooky spider webs.

When the room was decorated, I was asked to help. I had my sister come to help also. She loved the details: cutting out pumpkins and being in charge of detail, which suited her skills. She loved to sit at the table and rearrange decorations, pulling out fruit and leaves from a centre piece and making them look real. She was also called upon to reach high places in the room, the beams and above the windows. We used her height for good.

Once the room was complete we served a lunch which captured all the colours. We had a contest to see how many items of food and candy were fall colours. Most kids turned their nose up at turnips, (this made me laugh). The biggest winner was pumpkin pie. Many lists were brought forward for the prize. The winner was a girl in grade seven who had every item all the other contenders could think of, but she had one more, it was a strange looking squash from Mexico, that nobody else knew about.

We were commissioned to go to the green grocers after school to find it. The manager found it in a book of international food. We were so happy we did not have to disqualify it; I was so glad it was real.

The girl in grade seven was Fantasia, the sister of Felicia. I did not know that. It was great to offer up four huge pumpkin pies to the family of the winner. I was convinced I had not seen Felicia jump, skip and jump and skip so high. She was elated.

Chapter Six

My sister arrived home one school day in the early fall. She could not see the blackboard in class, relegated to the back of the room. She was not in trouble, she was just put in the back of the class because she was so tall.

"I just can't see the board," she explained to our Mom. It took her a few months to realize that no matter how large the teacher's printing became, she still could not see the blackboard. She had trouble knowing what she needed to do as an assignment.

It was a couple of weeks later, there was a notice that arrived home. Leanne was needing an eye check - up. She pronounced later she needed glasses. She was happy to report this because she could now see the blackboard in class, even at the back of the room. Her marks increased and she was a lot happier.

It was this event and others which helped her and all of us, when we had to solve some detailed and at times sinister problems in the neighbourhood.

Part Three

Chapter Seven

Mr. Wolk lived behind Mr. & Mrs. Hoek. He was silent and never spoke to anyone, but always watched the house where Mr. & Mrs. Hoek lived. He knew they had a daughter named Mary - Jane, but he was not interested in any children. He was not interested in anybody.

Mr. Wolk loved his backyard. It was cut short and perfectly gnawed, as though he had hired a goat to munch it even, much like Mr. Hoek.

The only difference between the two properties was the one Mr. Wolk owned was on an angle. His yard cut across the backyard of Claude Hoek. He constantly pointed out the little white posts which showed where both yards began and ended.

His concern was the children who did the plays were on his yard. He was not interested in the children once again, but only in the principle of where his yard started and ended.

This obsession became a thorn in the side of Claude Hoek. Claude talked to his wife about it and she smiled. Helen Hoek was the mother of Mary - Jane, and her eyes were only on her daughter. Helen did not care about a stupid yard dispute.

Mr. Wolk was hard working. He was outside in the brightest, hottest sun of the day, and worked until all hours of the night. Nobody cared about what he did. He had no visitors, no friends, no family that any one could relate to or see.

When he stood in the yard, he was stooped over. His face was old, and thin looking, and so was his hair. He was not that old himself, but his past life was unkind to him. When waved at, he declined. He was not amiable and would turn away when approached.

For the most part, the neighbourhood families ignored him. They knew he was a different sort, but passed no judgement. He did not bother them, so they did not bother him.

One day in early fall, Leanne decided to walk around the backyard where a play was staged the night before. She inadvertently stepped onto his grass right at the angle where both lawns met.

Mr. Wolk was out with a scythe in his hand. Leanne ran screaming to Mary - Jane`s house. She hid in the porch area where Claude Hoek stacked his wood for the winter.

Mr. Wolk advanced no further, but Leanne was scared out of her wits.

Later on we saw him using the scythe as if he was making a better path for her to follow. She was looking for a lost bracelet.

This image made Felix Wolk look like a scary person. I was not sure, yet what to think.

"Leanne, did Mr. Wolk say anything to you?" I was concerned.

"No, he didn't, but I was too scared to stay and listen." Leanne was adamant she was not going to go near him again.

From that event on we all watched Felix Wolk. As a group of kids we watched him from behind wood stacks, behind poles, or behind the few bushes which graced the fenced in area.

One day in early spring, I saw him with a cat. The cat was white with tiny black markings on its paws and tail. Mr. Wolk was petting it with so much love, I could not stop watching him.

"Leanne, look, he has a cat, which we have never seen before."

"Maybe, he keeps it inside during the winter, but now that it's fall, the cat is outside," she was trying to be calm, but I could sense the tension in her voice, as she watched.

"I wonder what he calls the cat?" I then went on to be a little daring. "I'm going to go and ask him."

"No, don't, because we are alone. If something happened to you over there, I wouldn't be able to help you." Leanne was trembling.

"He's just a lonely man. What can he do? He is so frail." I started walking over to his yard, much to the dislike of Leanne. When he heard me open and close the gate in between the yards, he turned. The cat meowed, like any cat, as soon as he stopped rubbing her belly.

When he looked up, his eyes gleamed with happiness and his face took on a whole new look. There was no denying it, he was happy to see me.

"Hi, my name is Stacey."

His voice was thin when he finally spoke. He said his name was Felix Wolk. I stood about two feet away from him

"What do you call your cat?"

"I have named her Chloe."

"That's a beautiful name for a cat." I wanted to get closer to pet her, but not sure how they would both react.

He stared at me for while, clearly not sure what to say.

I turned to see Leanne still standing at the gate. She was not able to bring herself to follow me.

"I live down the street towards the pool." I pointed to my sister. "That is my sister Leanne."

He didn't say anything, just nodded.

I turned and walked away. I could see Leanne breathing a sigh of relief, thinking she didn't have to rescue me in any way.

As we walked away toward the road, she pelted me with questions.

"Did he talk to you? Did he look happy or wicked? What was the name of the cat?" She continued on until I answered every question.

As we walked down the road to our house, I could not help thinking about Felix Wolk. Why did nobody on the street talk to him, befriend him, or even ask him over for coffee, lunch or dinner?

Leanne was talking as we walked together. I could barely filter what she was saying, my mind so intrinsically busy about this new event.

Little did I know there would be a lot of events like this one. Most good, but some sinister. I did not want to imagine the sinister ones, so I sat at the dinner table that night more quiet than talkative. My Mom asked why I was so serious. I put it off as a deep thought to a school assignment.

Chapter Eight

It was spring and all the pussy willows were in bloom. I could not believe how soft they were. The long stick like branches they grew from were up to the waist of most grade fours. We would pick their small, fuzzy white pods and use them in baskets as a soft blanket.

Some of us who had animals, would carry the baskets around with the soft lining inside. These baskets were home to kittens, gerbils, tiny dogs, baby rabbits and at one time little ducklings.

Our Mom would not allow us to have animals ever since Whitey our small terrier was injured, under the tires of a car, on the road right in front of our house. His leg was broken, but I remember, he survived, but for a long time was wearing a cast on his back, right leg.

Like I mentioned, Mom being sad at times, thinking about how she would have loved to have been a life guard, Dad would have loved to have had another dog. This was a bone of contention in the house. This was another reason there was mumbling at the table when Leanne and I tiptoed to our bedroom that night with our prized dessert. There was no way Mom would have consented to another dog, even after Whitey died, which was not long after he was run over. We think he had an internal injury as well as a broken leg.

There were other things to consider. With the air being warmer and now in the month of May, we were all anticipating the day we called May Day. This was an outside celebration at the school, where all students from various grades entertained the parents, who arrived on the school grounds for the day's celebrations.

As the older classes, we were delegated to be the performers in the Maypole dance. This was exactly as it sounded, a pole with students dancing around it.

I remember the flat field where we performed. Close to the corner of the school, and still able to be seen from the road. Every student in the May pole dance was given a long, long, ribbon. The long strands I thought at first were actually crepe, like the paper we used for crafts, but at a second look they were not easily ripped, they were probably some form of a ribbon like fabric.

The object was to have all the ribbons tied to the top of the pole first. I had no idea how that was done. The pole, probably twenty feet tall, would have had to be laid on the ground and all the ribbons fastened to the top.

When the pole was erected all the ribbons dangled down, one for each of the students in a class, to grab. If the colours for the ribbons were bright blue and yellow they would be staggered that way around the pole.

The grade fours for instance would have the yellow, and the grade fives would have the blue. The students would stand in a circle around the Maypole holding their designated ribbon. Once the music started one class would walk counter clock wise and the other would walk clockwise. When the music sped up, the students would skip.

The object now would be to make a basket weave starting at the top of the pole and weave down. This was accomplished by the students going in and out, then ducking up and under their opposing colours. As long as the dance stayed the same, the pattern stayed the same, and the weave would be accomplished.

I always thought this, was the greatest thing ever. It was so pretty when done, the results of many students working together to create something of beauty.

Once the finished product was viewed the viewer could see that every weave was yellow, and every second weave was blue. The last bit of ribbon in the hands of the students, at the bottom of the pole, were tied and fastened, so in a wind the whole thing would not become unravelled.

The rest of the day would be fun games on the field of grass and then of course, there were many booths of food set up all around the school yard.

I remember Mom would offer up her prized cinnamon buns and others would offer up food from the countries where they learned to cook. I remember the incredible dessert called Flan, from Mrs. Hoek. It was a superb dessert made in Holland, with a flat cake, sunken in the middle but filled with a scrumptious dessert, like peaches or apricots, with a white whipped, whipping cream on top. I cannot remember if there was a charge or not. My Dad loved this, especially, when we brought it home just for him. He always teased there was one bite missing.

I would always blame Leanne. She would get so mad at me.

"I did not." Meaning she did not steal a bite. Her response was:

"I would not steal a bite out of Dad's flan, but I would steal a bite out of yours, ha, ha."

The minute she said that, she saw my dessert sitting in my spot at the table. She ran over to it, fully intending on taking a bite. I beat her to the spot, then the fight was on.

We could then hear our Mother, "Now, you girls get along."

At dinner that night, we talked about Felix Wolk. Mom and Dad were quite surprised when I told them we visited Felix Wolk that afternoon.

"I pet his cat, which he named Chloe." I could tell Mom and Dad were a little concerned I had gone into his yard.

"Leanne would not go beyond the gate." I reiterated, trying to change the subject in a good way.

"He was left handed." Leanne, spoke, almost looking as though she too, wanted to change the subject.

Chapter Nine

Mom made a point of needing to speak to Mr. Wolk.

"Why is it, you need to speak to Felix Wolk?" My Dad was adamant that she not drag herself down there to have a chit chat, as much as she would like to.

"I will take a basket of buns or cinnamon buns, depending on the day and what I have baked. I will be asked to be invited into his house, and then offer him some of my baking." She was adamant again, about her plans.

When she became like this, Dad had no power. She was going to do whatever she had a mind to do. With Mom this meant now.

The day arrived and Mom baked cinnamon buns. We were at school still, when she sashayed over to visit Felix Wolk.

At the table that night we heard the details. He was kind, and offered her a seat in the house, when she arrived.

She then offered him the baking and he was intrigued by the sweet tasting cinnamon buns. He mentioned his Mom died when he was eight and his father remarried. He never felt special after that. He had never tasted cinnamon buns.

Mom continued on, "He grew up in Amsterdam. His family was small, but they had some special events together, which he remembered. He remembers missing his mother the most. The times he held her in his mind, were the most important times in his life.

Felix talked about his garden, his plants, his flowers, and the days he spent outside with his Mother, before she died of influenza. His life since then, and since the war have been difficult. He did say he was in love once in Amsterdam. Her name was Heleena."

Mom served dessert, her signature peaches, then she continued.

"When he arrived in Canada, he looked for a house. He still lives in that same house. He could not find his love from Amsterdam, even though he knew she had moved to Surrey, British Columbia, Canada. He was told she lived right around this area. He looked every day, but he did not find her, or know anyone that may know her. Her name was Heleena Van Stralen. He had searched the records, but to no avail."

The people at the records/archives stated many people with long, long names had their names changed to shorter ones when they arrived in Canada. This was because nobody could pronounce the long names of the immigrants. Felix was adamant, he indicated to the archives director that the last name Van Stralen was not that long or difficult to pronounce. He was sure it would not be shortened. He knew the front part of the name, Van, meant "from the house of" in Dutch, so that would have been the same. He was perplexed by all of it.

"I was happy, I had met Felix. I hope to see him again sometime. I was glad for the decision I made to visit, and to take over cinnamon buns." I could see Mom felt as though she was a good neighbour.

"Did you see the cat?" Leanne was anxious to hear about Chloe.

"I did," mom said. "It was pure white with tips of black on the tail and on its paws. It looked as though it ran through a spill of black paint.

I was not sure I liked the fact that Mom had met Felix Wolk. I could tell Dad was not happy about it either. She went against his wishes.

He had not met any other neighbours yet, even though he had lived there, almost forever. This made him appear a little odd, but a lot more isolated. "You know what happens to people who are isolated," I said out loud, "They go a little wacky. I wouldn't trust him."

Dad closed the subject by asking for brownies. Mom quickly rose and after picking up a three tiered, silver tray off the counter offered Dad an incredible banquet of baking: brownies, matrimonial cake, and fruit squares. Pineapple and coconut squares were also a favourite, and they graced the bottom of the three tier cake platter. Of course, there was also a copious amount of ice - cream; we went through so much ice - cream in that house.

The ice - cream during that time was a huge hit. I cannot remember how much it cost, but it was sold by the bucket. The bucket was a short white bucket, with a single metal handle.

The flavours were amazing. There was always vanilla, (which we had the most, because it went with everything), then there was chocolate, and many other buckets with flavours streaking through it, such as banana, mint, or cherry.

I remember those buckets were then washed out and used for any job under the sun. They were recycled for storing items such as dominoes, poker chips for card games, pennies for the game of Rummoli, and numerous other uses such as wash cloths and a cleaning bucket for scrubbing down the bathroom, one of Mom's favourite sayings.

When I realized the bucket was used to clean house, the idea of ice - cream withered a bit for me.

Not long after that evening meal, we were sitting watching T.V. and we heard a commotion outside.

When we saw what was happening, we jumped in without question. Outside in the front of the house, Felix was chasing a puppy which Leanne and I helped steer into a corner by the front porch.

"He got away, and now I am worried, he will not stay put." Felix, away from his back yard, and protection of his house looked lost. He was chasing his new puppy, and all Leanne and I could do was say, "Aww, he is so cute."

The puppy turned out to be a mixed breed, but it had floppy ears like a spaniel, and paws as big as a frying pan. I was stumped as to why Felix, would want to be training a puppy.

"He must be lonely," I thought. Quite a few weeks later, I asked him that same question. He said, he knew if he bought a puppy he would see the neighbourhood kids more often. He enjoyed our visit when we pet the cat.

Felix named the dog, Charlie. There was not a name game or ideas thrown around, it was just Charlie.

Charlie reeked havoc in his back yard, in his garden and in the house. Even the cat stayed away from him, until he grew up tall and large, but with the most gentle nature ever. Everybody loved Charlie. Luckily, Felix was strict with him and he was not allowed to bark, except if there was someone at the door, or apparent danger.

Charlie, would carry the cat, Chloe around in his mouth, only when Chloe allowed it. If she was not in the mood, she would scratch and hiss at him.

It was interesting to watch. Felix looked a lot younger since the dog arrived in his house and back yard. The dog became so big, Felix could not walk it, so he asked myself and Leanne to walk him, just down the side streets. Charlie grew to be eighty - four pounds and was also hard for Leanne and I to walk him. Mary - Jane sometimes helped if she was not taking piano lessons.

During that time, life went on in the area of Surrey. School was almost out for one more year, and we were making plans for a holiday. The Maypole was long gone, and the events around Mayday were also in the distant past.

Mary - Jane and Leanne were almost eleven and I was turning ten. We decided to go to a camp that summer. Our parents were a little worried, but not as worried as Mary - Jane's Mom and Dad, her being the only child and all.

The camp was close by, so if there were any issues with any one of us we would be picked up to go home.

I thought I would miss the neighbourhood, the plays, and the dog, Charlie and Chloe. Luckily, it was only for one week. When we were picked up by a truck full of other girls we helped them pack our small duffel bags and pillows into the back. The truck was already stuffed, but we managed to wedge everything in.

I will never forget the camp, the friendships, the camp fires, the songs, the smores and the times together. I knew after this trip, I wanted to be a leader, and lead children into becoming fun, educated and responsible adults. The leaders at this camp were amazing.

Leanne loved it as much as I did.

Part Four

Chapter Ten

Through the thick bars of his cell, Felix could see very little. He was alone again tonight. Other cell mates came and went. He wasn't sure where they were taken, but he didn't ask upon their return. He gave up nothing regarding himself. There was no telling if the guards were going to overhear, and use any bit of information against him or another prisoner.

Other than using the showers and walking in the yard, there was nothing to keep him occupied. It would have been nice to be able to talk to the others who were stuck there with him, but he knew and they knew, there was no reason to talk.

Felix fabricated events and days when he was a free man. He like any German Jew, was once free. His home was valuable, his business valuable, his family, more precious than all of it. His Mother died when he was young, and his father left to remarry, They were however, still precious in his mind. He had no siblings.

Before his father left, Felix remembered helping him in his shop. The most important thing to Felix was his father's approval, even though he knew him for only a short time. The family, which his father remarried into, kept his father busy. There were numerous children, however; Felix did not know them, or meet them. He was sent off to live with an aunt and his father never visited.

This and many other reasons made Felix sad, unhappy, and wishing he had a family to support him or care whether he lived or died. He made a pact with himself, he would never be alone again. He would create a family for himself, and have children. He would look for a woman to love, to marry and to be the loving Mother of his children.

The black iron bars clanked open and another prisoner was literally thrown into the cell. Felix stepped aside before the man tripped him, or he tripped the man.

The unruly guard gave an expletive that was less than flattering. Felix covered his mouth so he would not respond to it, and get himself into trouble. He witnessed many a prisoner mouthing back something to a guard. They were taken away and he never saw them again.

There was a good chance they were taken to the stockade which he found out by someone, having a nightmare in his cell one night, was not a place to be. The prisoner`s arms were stuck through wooden holes and they were trapped there.

Felix could not believe some of the stories he heard, just by listening to the ramblings of others. They were free with their information and they did not care who heard it.

He watched the two guards outside the cell. The cell door was securely locked, and now, besides himself there was another prisoner inside his small space. The area was six feet by six feet, barely enough room to walk in a circle. Two beds perpendicular to each other framed the walls, but that was it.

It was dark now. The faint, shimmer of light usually projected into the cell from the barred window was extinguished. The night was encroaching. On one bunk, the man who was recently thrown in, was making a lot of noise in his sleep. He had a throaty sound, and at times there was a muffled scream.

Felix had no idea what was making him scream, but then he decided he did not really want to know.

At midnight, two high ranking officers stepped into the hollow space outside his cell. He could see their faces in the dim light. They were young and eager, and he could see how they wanted to be big in the regime. Not only were they dressed for a high ranking position, but their talk was nothing but what they were going to do, when they reached an even higher rank.

Felix knew he could divulge of their conversation, but he dare not. He would be the one killed, not them. He knew they were planning to murder the men at the top of the regime and stage a coup.

When Felix coughed he asked for water. One of the men looked annoyed, quickly opened the cell door and thrust him a glass of water. It was a tin cup, glass would be a weapon.

As soon as the cup was given, there was a whistle outside. Felix could tell the two officers he was watching, were being summoned. He waited to see what was going to happen.

Both men jumped up and ran outside. Apparently, there was a prisoner exchange.

Felix moved closer to the cell bars which served as a gate. He leaned forward more than usual, to see what he could see through the diminishing light. To his surprise the cell door moved a fraction. Felix put his hand up to the bar, and pushed with his palm. The cell door moved out even more and then he had to make a decision.

When the two men were initially in the space outside his cell, they were looking at a sheet of paper. Two men of high ranking order buzzing over a list of higher ranking men. Felix heard this and wondered why they had it.

Maybe they confiscated it to see who the high ranking men were, they had to outsmart.

Felix moved the bar door open just enough to etch his body through it. He stepped out to freedom, but instead of just dodging away, he had to make a decision.

Felix, not only would try to escape the camp, but he would escape the camp with the paper he saw lying there on the table.

Rolling the paper up quickly, he hid it in his underwear and then looking around one last time, left the compound. It was pitch black, without a soul in sight. All the officers were marshalled in a muster area on the other side of the field. He was totally alone.

When Felix saw the position he was in, he grinned. He knew this event at night would take more than an hour; he had witnessed it before from his cell. He looked up at his sentries; they were facing the crowd in the muster area.

Felix slipped through the trees leading to the forest and stealthily moved away as fast as he could.

He knew that the breaking, more like the snapping of dry twigs could be heard by the sentry. That was how the last escapee was caught, so he walked zigzag through the forest only on soft ground covered in pine needles.

The last thing Felix wanted was to be chased by a man with a high powered gun. He could not fathom that and decided to look back more often. Nobody was following him.

Luckily, Felix paid attention to any maps he had placed in front of him over the years, at school, at his aunt`s house, and in the prison library. He remembered how close the border was, from Germany to Holland.

As soon as the forest ended, Felix saw a small village, and decided to find something he remembered seeing in black and white movies. He was looking for a clothes line. He had in mind, a pair of pants, old sweater and a hat. His idea was to disguise himself, and find a burying hole for his prison clothes.

He found what he needed on a clothes line, in a back lane. He whisked the clothes off the line, just in time to see and hear a German lady running after him, with what looked like a rolling pin. She had on an apron, and looked as though she was baking something.

As Felix ran, his mouth started to water thinking of the pie, or cake, or German Flan she may have been baking.

The forest was deep and long, but after all his map reading Felix knew where to cross the border between Germany and the Netherlands.

When it felt safe enough for him to stop and catch his breath, he stripped off his prisoner clothing, buried them deep under a tree root, put on the clothes pilfered from the

German lady and started walking, then running. He was pleased the clothes were almost his size, including the hat.

There was a knock on the door. ``Where was he``

He knew there were no doors to knock on in the forest. He looked up, his front door was definitely making a noise.

`Felix, can we come in to pet the cat and play with the dog?`` Stacey needed to see the animals. It seemed like a long time without them.

He looked around, he was home. He had been dreaming.

"Just a minute." Felix moved slowly to the door, his head still, in a dazed state.

When he arrived at the door, he turned the wooden handle and was surprised to not only see Stacey, but Leanne.

The minute he opened the door, both girls entered.

Leanne was scared to death. She immediately ran around to blow out all the candles which were lit in the living room and in the kitchen. All the candles were white, short, and looked as though they had been used over and over. Down each candle stick, wax had cooled into globs, making the whole room look like a séance.

"Felix, why all the candles?" Stacey helped Leanne with the candles which were closest to her.

"Oh, I don't know. I am just used to having them from many years ago." Stacey, walked over and gave him a hug. She knew he was thinking about the times when he was younger.

It was dark now and all the windows were shadowed. Felix went around closing the shutters.

"Were you girls needing something?" He still felt confused.

"We just wanted to pet Chloe and play with Charlie."

Felix then looked at the clock and realized both animals had missed their dinner. He wasn‘t sure how long he slept, but it was long enough for him to forget his duties.

"I will show you where the cat and dog food bins are so if I ever fall asleep again you may come in and feed them."

"Try not to have so many lit candles Felix. If the dog or cat ever bumped a table the candles could be on the floor and the house could be on fire." Leanne, always the voice of reason, stared at him, to make sure he was listening. He was.

He was kind. He loved them more now, than he ever thought he could. He was so happy he chose a cat and dog to share the household. This household was not only shared by animals but shared by children.

Stacey and Leanne filled the bowls, filled the water dish, took the dog out to the yard for a run and then returned.

When the door closed Felix lay down again and dreamed.

He was back in the forest.

He was running and running hard now. His mind was on one thing. How is he going to cross the border without papers? He had not thought this through. Where was he going to go, even if he managed to slip through somehow? Holland was close, he could tell by the building at the border and the Dutch flag.

There were many line ups of people. They were crossing into Holland with wheelbarrows and shovels and brown parcels tied up with string, packaging all of their belongings.

Stopping outside the arena of the busiest border crossing, Felix had to make a decision. Even if he had papers to show, they would recognize his name. By now any authority would be looking for an escaped inmate. He started to worry.

He had to make a decision once again, right on the spot. As his mind was working fast, his body was slowly moving to the right, using every tree for cover. He kept moving, his feet sliding side - ways and his body following without mentally, realizing it.

He was heading towards the hills. He could not join the line ups; he could not stand there. He had to be gone. He had to be gone away from eyes and authority, and any means of being recognized.

Back in school, many years ago, Felix remembered reading maps about this border. He remembered being astounded at how long the border was, and how the landscape changed. Once it was flat and then stubby with grass, he looked up and sure enough in the distance, small rising hills took over the horizon. He stopped. Those were the hills he had remembered from the maps. There were many of them and they were famous for hiking with numerous winding, nature trails.

"That's it, that's where I need to go. Hide in the mountains, hide where nobody else, would need to go. Find my way there, and look for rivers and streams. Find berries to eat, and fish in the rivers."

There was a loud noise. It was the siren. The siren that all people in the camp were afraid of the most. A missing inmate. All guns were out, and the guards were running full speed. He could not see anyone, luckily, he was far enough away.

"It would just be my luck," Felix thought. "The woman in the village would be able to recognize the clothes he took, including the hat and they would have a sight on him soon."

The next tree was only a short space away. He side stepped into it and then rolled on the ground. Absolutely nobody could see him now, he was that close to the base of the rolling hill. He could make it. He did.

The side of the rolling hill was full of tall grass. He was more than thankful for this. Now, all he needed to do was climb. His ability to climb was excellent, but he was becoming weak. He could not remember the last time he had eaten.

Climbing up the rolling hill through the tall grass gave him a chance to duck down and look at the line ups below him. So far, there were no guards trailing him.

He climbed higher. There was a small breeze which helped him feel more alive, more energetic and more hopeful. Along the way, Felix found shrubs full of berries and without even thinking he grabbed a bunch and shoved them into his mouth. This was the extra energy he needed. They were sharp, sweet, and juicy.

While climbing and enjoying the berries at each level, he suddenly heard it; the noise every inmate fears.

Looking down from the summit for the last time, Felix could now see the ground pummeled with the colour of the guard's uniforms, and hear shots being fired. After the shots, there were screams from the people in the line up.

Nobody had seen him, so the people in the line up did not have to lie, or look like they were lying. The guards were able to sense when a person was lying right away.

The noise outside was deafening. Stacey and Leanne were striking a huge bell. They thought it was funny, and kept striking it. Their Mom had come to fetch them for dinner. They had been doing a play practice. She immediately grabbed the stick they were banging the bell with and scooted them along home.

Felix grabbed Chloe and put his hand on the head of Charlie, and realized he was safe. There was no one here, no one in a guard's uniform and no shots being fired.

He was so thankful, he got up and started making dinner.

Chapter Eleven

The last thing Felix wanted was the neighbourhood kids knowing he was an inmate, during the war. He knew it wasn't his fault, yet he felt stained by it.

He wanted to be real, to be available to them without having to explain everything. He also knew one day the explaining would come. kids were curious; they deserved to know the truth.

However, they didn't need to know right now There would be a waiting period where kids heard the facts at the right time. Felix could wait, he knew waiting was part of his life. Had he not spent a large part of his life, waiting already? Waiting to be released from prison, waiting to find the love of his life.

These kids didn't know who he was or what he had been waiting for. They were young, they did not need to know the agony of waiting. Once Felix figured this out, it was easier to exist in the neighbourhood. He did not have to lie. He would wait for the right time to tell the truth.

Summer was over, fall was over and life went on. The young people of this neighbourhood went to school in the rain and never complained. They were use to the rain; it was Surrey, British Columbia.

Mrs. Hoek stood outside on the porch each morning, still blowing her nose. She continually blew her nose on the front porch and watched the end of the street, until every school child went through the front door of the school building. Only then, did she start her chores.

Mr. Hoek today was driving to the airport. He was picking up his nephew, Horace Hoek. Horace was forty years old, never married, lived all his life in Holland, and was now here in Canada, on a case. He was a detective.

Claude Hoek was a great admirer of his nephew. There was something truthful and real about Horace, Claude could not put his finger on it, but he had a feeling. The feeling was more of an intuition. Claude recognized talent and Horace had the gift. Horace had the gift to be an inquisitive and excellent detective.

Mary - Jane was intrigued by Horace. When he walked up the two rickety steps to the house she was in full view of him where she was standing at the front room window.

Horace took her hand once he entered the house, like a princess. She felt his invisible kiss on the back of her palm and that was the moment she became shy, and as she voiced to Stacey and Leanne, she was in love.

Yes, Horace was a good looking guy. He had dark hair, a small dark beard and brilliant blue eyes. He was not quite six feet tall, but the most noticeable characteristic about Horace was his kindness and gentleness. Mary - Jane had never heard a voice so melodious, so soft, especially coming from a man. Although, she was quite aware she had not known or heard too many men speak in all of her eleven years, but she knew, he was special.

Helen Hoek was the perfect hostess. She had been baking forever since she knew he was coming.

"How was the flight?" Her questions were short. She also, was shy, like Mary - Jane. Her English was good, but she felt more comfortable speaking Dutch.

"It was excellent." Horace spoke softly in English. He had an incredible accent, the first thing Mary - Jane noticed.

When he spoke in Dutch to her Mother, it was then, Mary - Jane wished she could speak her parent's language.

"Do not worry little one, I will teach you." Horace was staying for at least four months, so Mary - Jane knew she had a chance to learn at least conversational Dutch. She heard the word conversational from her French teacher. She picked up languages quickly.

He also admitted he wanted to teach her how to play chess. She was pumped.

Claude was so pleased to have another male figure in the house, he could not do enough for Horace. He showed him his room, and then the back yard, and then the wood shed, and also the shop. He knew Horace along with himself, would find countless hours in these places for quiet talk and of course the business Horace was there to do.

When Mary - Jane went to school the next day, the talking began. Horace was over for numerous reasons. He wanted to see his family, he wanted to visit Canada, but he also had a job to do.

There was a secret job he was commissioned to do, whereby even his uncle was not able to learn of it. There were other detective jobs they were both working on together. They learned of spies in and around the country, but nothing had materialized as yet. On the air, numerous espionage channels were secretly devised, but nobody suspected any serious complications – yet.

This era, a decade after the second world war, was still ripe with events needing to be kept secret, but watched. The last thing all the diplomats in any country wanted was another war ignited.

"So, uncle, tell me what you are hiding under this wood pile. Is it a secret hiding place with a trap door or a place for all your Dutch beer?" Horace had a passion for his country. Everything he thought about had to do with the Dutch people.

"No, nephew, I wish it was a stash, but Helen does not believe in a drinking man, and don't forget we have a young lady in the house looking to us for security and good morals. She is a blessing to us."

"She is lovely, uncle, I can see her growing into a mature young woman, whom any family would be proud." Horace tapped Claude on his shoulder.

"I will be happy to teach her our mother tongue. She will be able to converse by the time I leave." Horace felt confident about his skills.

Claude could hear his wife calling both of them from the kitchen. Dinner was ready, so they stepped into the backyard, went through the back door, and sat down. It was great to cook for four, Helen had stated, the minute she saw all four chairs filled up. She had always wanted a larger family, but she was grateful for what she had.

Once the food platters were handed around the table, Horace asked a couple of questions to Helen and then to Mary - Jane.

"Helen," he said, what is this soft, puffy bun shaped like a chef's hat and filled with gravy?"

"They call it Yorkshire Pudding in Canada. It was originally from England, but Canadians like it a lot." She lowered her eyes.

"Stacey and Leanne have it at their house more than we do." Mary - Jane was keen to offer up what she knew about her friends and their love for the dish. "When their mom cooks it the whole house smells like grease. Stacey jumps up and down when she comes home from school and knows what's for dinner just by the hot smell."

"So, Mary - Jane I have a question for you." Horace turned his chair a bit to her side. "What is your favourite subject in school?"

Mary - Jane felt honoured to be asked a personal question. It showed how much a person is respected when someone is interested in their life.

"I love math, and I also love learning another language. In Canada most students learn to speak French." She smiled and then coughed.

"If you have learned how to speak one language, you will find it easy to learn another." Horace was appealing to her senses, believing she takes her education seriously.

"Tell me what you love about math?" He had an idea in his mind which took math into account.

"I fell in love with math, when I had a great teacher. I love the symmetry of it, the prime numbers, and how math is never wrong."

"If you love the symmetry of it, the strict pattern of its own rules, you will love the game of chess." Horace saw her face light up.

"I know I will love it. There is a small chess club at school, but so far very few feel confident to join. Maybe, Uncle Horace you could join us and help us at school, even one noon hour a week."

"I would love that."

The rest of the dinner hour went by quickly. Helen had an over zealous dessert which everyone partaked. It had many colours: red raspberry, blueberries, and chocolate drizzled all over vanilla ice cream.

Claude sat back with his pipe and grinned. "Now this is a family."

Chapter Twelve

It was almost spring. The pussy willows were in full bloom and the apple blossom trees were magnificent in their wardrobe of white and pink.

Felix could not believe how the children in the neighbourhood carried baskets around on their arms lined with soft, white pussy willows for miniature animals. They carried little ducklings, bunnies, and kittens. The only problem was, the little creatures wanted to jump out as soon as they were set down.

He knew, the reason he noticed this now, was due to his cat Chloe, and his puppy Charlie. If he had not thought to have pets, he would never have met the children of the neighbourhood. This was the greatest development since he moved to his house.

However, Felix was still looking for his past love, whom he met in Amsterdam, years ago. He was also looking for freedom from his dreams, in some cases night mares. After Stacey and Leanne left from helping him feed and walk Charlie, then cuddle Chloe, he fell asleep on his couch, once again.

He was tromping through the forest. The gun shots had lessened and his ears were popping from the previous sounds. He could see through the tall grass, all the soldiers were gone. He felt relieved. His legs felt as though they were filled with cement. It was a large climb to the top of Vaalserberg. If his incredible memory helped him this hill was 322 m. the highest peak in Holland. This landscape structure, marked borders on Belgium, Holland and Germany. Tall coniferous trees, bracken ferns with triangular shaped fronds littered the trail. Felix was more than happy to remember the location of this famous hill and he felt for the first time in a long time, a closeness to Mother Nature.

He patted his upper pants still feeling the rolled up piece of paper he stole from the two guards. Once again, as in the past twenty – four hours he was happy the guards did not connect with him and up to now, he has been free.

The only problem was, he was not sure what would happen next. Where would he go, what would he do, and primarily, what would he do with the paper he stole?

Felix, was all alone, and in this instance not sure how to proceed for his own protection, and to whom would he entrust the valuable piece of paper, currently tickling his waistband?

He found more berries as he ascended. He was pleased it was spring and not the dead of winter.

He ate all the berries he could find without achieving a stomach ache. As he climbed he saw rabbits scurrying here and there. He decided to look for shelter and then put up a snag for a rabbit. His own sense of delirium made him want to stop.

Not far from his trodden path he spotted a cave like structure. Picking up a long, sharp stick he poked his way into the dark cave. The cave entrance had a large flat rock on top. It appeared as though there was no creature in residence, so he ventured in.

The moment he was able to start a fire, he felt warmer and less exposed inside the rock dome. Picking up flint along the way, helped him to create a spark. He also had twigs and moss to contribute to the fire.

Little did he know, he escaped just in time into the cave like dwelling and did not see a group of guards slither by his entrance. Luckily, he had the common sense to create his fire hidden away from the opening of the cave. When it appeared safe he stole out to set a trap for a rabbit and to collect larger pieces of wood.

Felix felt enchanted, and with the rabbit circling on the spit he knew his long, ignored hunger would be satiated. His next move would be: where to hide the rolled up paper in his pants waistband and to make sure he would find it many years later, if need be.

Night was encroaching. After a good meal and a little nap, Felix woke up to a pitch black cave and the need to carry on.

He did just that.

Marching down the huge hill he realized he was still free and safe.

This was the freedom he predicted all those days in his cell. Once he reached the bottom of the hill in the pitch blackness he could breathe again.

He found a place amongst the ferns to sleep. His breathing lowered and his energy returned.

Just before sunrise he awoke. He had to climb out of his state and determine where to go next.

The answer was right in front of him. He saw a huge number of people walking over a small footbridge between Germany and Holland. He walked right into Holland with no guards and no need of custom papers. With his clothing and hat, he looked like any worker going to a job who would be wearing work clothes much like his.

When he saw the village and the shops he whistled for joy. There were no more guards to worry about and there was no more fear.

He was fed and given a two-day sleep on a cot from a non-profit society; he knew one day he would pay it back.

After a good rest, and plenty of food, Felix found a place to settle into and worked his room and board off with chopping wood, hauling water, falling trees and carrying lumber to others who were no longer able to do physical work.

In between working hard to stay alive Felix found time to explore the hills. Along with the Vaalserberg hill Felix found something else. He found a cabin. This cabin was in such disrepair it was hard to figure someone would be living in it.

After visiting the cabin five times, he was convinced nobody was coming back. It was at this time he made a decision. He was going to hide his rolled up paper somewhere in the cabin, or around the cabin.

His decision was right. The cabin was deserted and at this elevation the chances of anyone wanting to come back to live there were preposterous.

The last hike Felix took up the mountain to this designated place, he stayed.

He decided to move the rough timber out of the cabin, build a fire and make it home. There were no dishes or amenities for future comfort, but he decided to make it home anyway.

He found a tree with a dark hole in it for his paper, and a deep hole in the log cabin chink. He had to decide soon. Where was he going to hide this piece of paper, he so grudgingly held onto?

In the dark hole in the tree was a great idea, and at first it seemed the best idea, however, a flash of safety ran through him one morning. He knew the tree could be attacked by insects or even a woodpecker. He wasn't too sure if there were woodpeckers in this country, but he was well aware of noises which sounded exactly like it. He was also worried about fire and /or lightning. At any time the tree could go up in flames simply from mother nature alone.

Looking around the rustic cabin Felix thought of another plan. There were loose bricks on the back wall. Taking one brick out at a disadvantaged height he noticed a long slim space going back into the wall. He tried the paper rolled up into it and the fit was perfect.

Putting the brick back made the wall look finished and not tampered with at all. This would be the spot.

Over his journey Felix had taken the paper out of his waistband many times and over many days he had started to memorize the names on the sheet. There were twelve. They were all German names, however, after numerous days in his cell, he was able to recognize the German language. He not only recognized the language but he recognized the names of the high officials on the sheet.

If years later, he were to hear anything about the Regime he would be able to not only pronounce the names on the sheet of paper, but able to recognize a picture or any of the twelve men.

He made a pact with himself. He would never tell anyone what he knows, what he has found out and where the paper is hidden. Felix put the paper back into the long space he found, placed the brick over it and after five weeks of being in the cabin; he left.

It was late spring and the grass had grown on his back lawn, a thick green. He decided to go out with his scythe and attack the tallest blades. He tried to do this when Stacey and Leanne were in school. He remembered when he scared Leanne that day with the scythe, even though he didn't know she was looking for a lost bracelet.

Felix finished the tallest grass and went in for lunch. He noted there was something different about the house adjacent to his yard. Claude and Helen had been entertaining a guest. He looked young, but Felix had no idea who he was. He knew, however, as soon as Stacey and

Leanne, and even Mary - Jane were home from school, they would tell him anything he wanted to know.

This was the only way he knew the names of Helen and Claude; the kids told him.

This was new to him. He spent years alone, not talking to anyone and now the children want to come over all the time to see Chloe and Charlie.

Felix could see the top of the man's head, he had dark hair, cut well, and a dark well trimmed beard. He looked official. Felix was anxious to know all about him. He just had to wait a few more hours for the kids to arrive home.

After lunch Felix felt weary and took a nap. His dreaming continued. His place of residence had changed. He was no longer in the cabin high up in the Vaalserberg hills in Holland. He had found a small place after the war, in a rooming house. They were popular then, not so much now. The rooming house had a store on the main floor.

The kind people who owned the building gave him work in their store. He knew the language well and was good with numbers. The couple had a daughter about his age. Her name was Heleena Van Stralen.

She was a beauty. He could not get her off his mind, during his work day, at dinner, all evening at home, and then all weekend. When he wasn't working, he was in pain. She eclipsed any other thought in his head, until the days were pure agony.

Her parents knew he had no money, no future and so he had chosen to not make a plea for her, afraid of being turned down. This day at work was like any other.

"Felix," Hans called in his strong Dutch brogue. He looked up and saw a huge sight on the main street. This sight stopped everyone in their tracks. They were not used to strangers walking in their village. These men were Germans from the past. They were dressed up to look official, and everyone moved away quickly. The war was over, but there was still terror in the hearts of all the people in Holland.

Felix bowed out of the store quietly, without being noticed. He was determined not be spotted, to ruin his life now that he was free.

"What if they have pictures of him?" he thought. He thought again, the war was over, he need not worry.

In the back of the store numerous sacks of grain and numerous pots of dirt were stacked high. The store sold all types of items from food to flowers. In Holland, the population of flowers became part of every household in the spring. Fields and fields of flowers sprouted all over Holland, mostly tulips and daffodils. It was this height which kept Felix from seeing Heleena. She was tall, but where she was working, stacking product, she was hidden.

Felix could hear the pounding of the boots coming into the store. There were three men, six pounding boots reverberated on the cement floor. He could hear every sound from the back of the store.

He could hear them hollering at Heleena's father. "I have no one here, who was an escapee. Why are you here, and why are you asking?" Hans was starting to shake and Heleena recognized this. His voice was wobbly and weak. She started to move to the front of the store, away from her place of work at the back. As soon as Felix noticed this, he sidled up to her. He put his arm on her arm and whispered in her ear. "These men are cruel and evil. We must be quiet and hope they go away."

Heleena was smart enough to not question or argue the point. She stood breathless. It was then the three men with resounding boots started to walk towards the back of the store. Felix was an expert on noise and noise placement over all those years, all he did was listen. He knew they were coming in.

"Heleena, when the men come in, do not be alarmed. I am going to kiss you when they come to us. The German's seem to cower at this outward affection and they will leave. Please do not show alarm, when I do this. We must look like we are in love and are finding a secret spot for our admiration." Her blue eyes gave full understanding.

When the German men snooped through the back room, they were surprised to see two young people arm in arm, lips locked and not even hearing them.

They all left laughing, saying the words in German about kissing, love and many other words Felix was glad nobody understood, including Heleena, and her father. All three were happy when the interlopers left. From that moment on, Felix was more smitten than ever. He breathed a sigh of relief.

Heleena walked away with red spots on her cheeks. Felix said nothing; he was breathless.

Chapter Thirteen

It was shortly after this event, Heleena was gone for good. Felix had no way of knowing where or why, and Hans could not give details.

Felix was beside himself. Even if he knew the reason, it would not matter, she was still gone.

Over the years, Felix stayed with Hans and his wife, Heleena came home twice. She smiled at him a lot, but looked disinterested. It wasn't until five years passed when Felix found out the real truth.

Heleena had been badly beaten by strangers in her own village. The strangers were never found or caught. Hans only wished for his daughter to have the best of everything. The best education, the best chances for a career, and the best life, hopefully with a family one day. The last Hans heard, she was living with an aunt in Canada.

This prompted Felix to find a passage to America. He searched on the water every day for a vessel to "stow" him across the ocean. He took every minute of his spare time to search for a vessel which would offer him passage to the United States or Canada. He knew when he got off the ship in the United States it was closer to Canada than Holland.

He had to act fast. This latest news was heart lifting. He wanted to find her before someone else found her, and she became married. The ships were in the harbour. Felix was granted "stow away" status on a vessel only when he offered up a large portion of his life savings, to a needy captain.

After saying good-bye to Hans and his wife, Felix gave them a large portion of his savings as well, and he was gone.

He woke up from this particular dream to the noise of Charlie barking at his front door.

Charlie and Choe were both making noise. Charlie was barking at the kids who were trying to get in, and Chloe was making purring noises to be fed.

"Felix, come out, it's sunny." Leanne was prompting him to get off the couch and get some sun. She was all about nurture and nature.

"Stacey is already throwing the ball for Charlie to catch." Leanne helped him with his sweater and out they went.

When Stacey first saw Felix, her voice was all about the plays in the summer. "Soon there would be practices and shows on the back lawn." She smiled at him widely.

He relished it. She wanted him to be aware this event was going to be happening soon. She did not want him surprised, if he fell asleep on his couch, and there were kids making noise outside.

"So, where is Mary - Jane? Who is the fellow that is her guest?" Felix questioned. "He has been in their house for a long time."

Felix chose to not step out further, until he knew who the strange man was in their house. Over the years, he had been nervous about strangers, due to his past and the fears he had lived through all his life. This was one reason he was a recluse, and did not trust people. Somehow, he trusted kids and dogs.

As the sun found its way to the side of his face and his clothing started to warm up, Felix could only think of his past dream. He was right at this moment thinking of Heleena. He wished with all his heart he could find her.

One day soon, he would find out where she is living. Hans has now been deceased for the better part of a year and his wife shortly after. They never did find out the exact location of their only daughter. The Aunt had also been deceased so Felix was on his own to discover the whereabouts of Heleena. Only a good detective could do that, but Felix knew it was extremely costly.

When Mary - Jane arrived in the back yard to pet the animals, she was her age and more. She was only eleven, but she looked like she may have been fourteen. The man in the house had been giving her lessons in Dutch and lessons in chess. She had risen to the occasion appearing brighter, smarter and had gained a higher degree of confidence.

She enticed Stacey and Leanne at school to sit in on the chess lessons being given, and they too appeared brighter and more confident.

"So, Mary - Jane who is the tall gentleman living in your house?" Felix asked in a friendly manner, shying away from sounding nosy.

``He is my uncle Horace from Amsterdam." She was more than proud when she said this. Felix wondered why.

"How long will he be staying?"

Mary - Jane mentioned four months, but she heard earlier that week, if he did not complete his mission, it would be longer.

Felix could feel his skin crawl a little. His body had reacted. He knew this was a sign of something, years ago, he felt this same strange feeling. Just then something would happen to make him believe there was a warning sign in all of this.

``He is a detective. His reason for being here is he is working on a case from the war. My dad is his brother, and they are working on something together. I think it's top priority, they can't tell us.``Mary - Jane stopped so she wouldn't reveal any more details.

Felix all of a sudden felt ill. He had nothing to worry about, but the past came hurtling back to him. His face blanched and at this time Leanne took him inside to lie down. He did not want to dream or go back in time, so he sat up quickly, and asked for a glass of water.

``Would you like to meet my uncle?" Mary - Jane asked. She had helped Leanne take Felix into the house and sit him on the couch.

"Maybe one day." Felix knew it would not be today. His head was spinning and after the sip of water, he lay his head on the back of the sofa, and closed his eyes. The girls tiptoed out.

When Mary - Jane talked at the dinner table that night she had a lot to say about Felix. Horace did not know there was a man in the back yard, and who spoke with an accent. When he asked Claude what language Felix spoke, Claude did not know, but Helen did.

``How do you know?`` Claude was curious.

"I have heard him speak to the cat and the dog in two other languages."` Helen was proud to say it was Dutch and German.

Horace could not believe they had never talked to the man in the back yard or had him over for something to eat or drink. This was not Dutch hospitality, he thought. He knew they were hospitable, because they were letting him stay with them as long as he needed to, in their own home. Extending hospitality was universal, but it was more difficult for strangers who were shy and reclusive.

It was a few days later when Horace saw Felix in the back yard with Chloe and Charlie. Helen was hanging clothes out on the line. It had metal pulleys to force the clothing out over the yard. The two metal clothes lines with pulleys squeaked, loudly.

Claude was gone for the day, and all the children on the street were in school. Horace watched Felix from a hidden advantage point, from the porch at the back of the house. Horace could see how he was bent over, how slowly he walked around his yard, and how his fine, thin hair became whipped up by the wind. Even with these characteristics he did not appear that old.

The constant, sultry squeaking of the clothesline made it hard to concentrate, but there were things Horace was interested in regarding Felix Wolk. He learned his last name from Claude and Helen. It was odd, he noticed,

Helen kept watching him. It was as though she knew him, or wanted to know him. Horace thought about what he already knew, and what he had heard about Felix.

Apparently, Mary - Jane's friends down the street had reached out to him first, and then their mother had visited. She had taken over cinnamon buns, and he was extremely grateful. He offered her a seat in his living room. Stacey and Leanne were allowed to visit him now, because the mother gave her consent. He was lonely, but harmless.

When Felix decided to be a pet owner, adopting Chloe and Charlie from the pound, this opened up huge possibilities for the girls and for Mary - Jane. All three girls now had pets to feed, to walk, to cuddle and Felix had the best time of his life. He was never privileged to know young children, but now they were a huge blessing to him.

"I wonder what his life was like before? I would love to hear about his journey and where he came from. It has been told that he lived and worked in Amsterdam. I wonder where he lived and worked in the city?" Horace knew Amsterdam well, just arriving from there a month ago. He had lived there since he was a boy.

He knew one day soon he would wander over and introduce himself to Felix. Right now he was focusing on his volunteer work at the school, teaching intermediate children how to play chess. Horace also had a secret life nobody knew about, he was one of many, looking for men from the war. He could not even tell Claude what his mission was, as it would only take a conversation heard by an outsider to have a wanted person skip the country. It was still not many years after the war, and there was still a lot of secrecy and espionage.

Little did Stacey, Leanne and Mary - Jane know what happened before they were born, and Horace hopes they will never know the tragedies of war.

Chapter Fourteen

With the children in school, Felix had just the dog and cat for company. They were both asleep in their cozy circular beds. Felix loved the way the dog stared at him, then his eyes would close and then the cat would look at both of them.

With the fire on, the room was warm; it was a perfect spring day, time to have a nap. Felix got up to lock the door, he was and always would be cognizant of safety, with no one taking him by surprise. He knew when the children arrived however, they were chatty and their footsteps were small, not like big boots.

The flames were high and the room overly heated, but not one sound erupted from Felix or the animals. Felix went back in time, as his eyes closed, he found himself, once again in a dream.

He was on the ship. The ship he found which would "stow" him away, was a relic. He was obliged to give the needy captain a large sum of money. If the ship was stopped and a stow away found on board the whole ship would be lost and the captain charged.

In return for the money, Felix was given a place to hide and two meals a day. His quarters were under the life boats on the farthest edge of the ship. He had to watch through crevices any time some one came on board, in his vicinity. He knew silence was the number one issue.

Felix also knew the journey was long. In those days it depended on the ship: the age of the ship, the speed of the ship, and if it had to make any stops, to unload, to fuel up, or if it needed a harbour.

The journey was nothing compared to the excitement he felt about trying to find Heleena. In the farthest reaches of his back pack he had a letter. This was the last letter given to Hans before he died of influenza, along with his wife. The aunt, Heleena was living with, finally wrote and told her story about how she was deathly ill, and how she had left the house to Heleena. Later on in the letter, Hans and his wife found out Heleena had to sell the house to live. She worked, but there was too much expense. This was how Felix learned she had moved to a small apartment type dwelling in Surrey, British Columbia, Canada.

However, after many years of looking to no avail, Felix still had not located his true love from Amsterdam. He thought over all the years, she must have married and changed her name.

The archives could not find her even with her maiden name of Van Stralen. He was bitterly disappointed. He begged them to look again. They kept repeating the same fact. Names were shortened when all the immigrants landed in the Americas. Felix did not believe the name Van Stralen could be shortened any further. If the "Van" part was taken off it would be an insult to the Dutch, as it was a signature part of any Dutch name.

Nevertheless, Felix was undaunted. Now, that he was older, did it really matter? He spent a lot of his time in jail oversees, so now he just wanted to enjoy the children who lived beside him and then the upcoming plays. It was such a joy to be blessed with energetic children around him and now pets.

But he was still dreaming. He started to rock back and forth. The ship was rocking back and forth. They had hit a storm. He lunged for Charlie and Chloe. He made them sit with him on his couch. In his mind he was hugging himself on the ship. The relic tossed and turned. Now water was flowing into the area he used to sleep in.

He woke up, worried his bedding would be destroyed, and there would be no blankets for the cold, cold night.

The front door was bristling with activity. The girls were now shouting to come in. He hollered "Just a minute, just a minute."

When they exploded through the door the light from outside burned his eyes. The fire in the fireplace had calmed down and Felix realized he was not on the ship. He was safe at home in Canada, with the children and his pets.

He hugged each girl with Chloe in his arms. His eyes started to become moist, and all three girls stared at him.

"It's okay, Felix, we love you too."

They all moved together for a group hug and that's how the time after each school day, started. They all enjoyed the company of each other, and the warmth it brought.

As soon as the group hug was over they raced Charlie out the front door with a bone and a ball and the noise became louder and louder.

Felix was still dazed from his last dream, so he walked slowly over to the garden bench and sat down. The green garden bench with scrolled iron along its sides was now brought out of hiding from the garage, and Felix loved it.

He could sit and watch. He revelled in watching the kids run and play with the dog, and chase the ball.

No sooner had he sat down when he noticed a tall man walking towards him. He recognized this man, with dark hair and a well kept beard. As soon as Horace walked closer, Mary - Jane went into action. She wanted Horace to meet Felix.

Horace wanted to meet Felix also, so Mary - Jane, took it upon herself to introduce the two of them.

Felix stood up and walked towards Horace and even before Mary - Jane could introduce them they shook hands.

Both men conversed in Dutch for a short while. After Mary - Jane introduced them properly, Horace put his arm around his niece and then she left looking for Charlie's bone in the yard.

Both men now sat on the bench. There was a small amount of tension, but not much. Horace did not want it turning into an inquisition, so he kept the chatter light.

Felix, was also curious, but wanted the visitor to start the conversation first. After their small talk in Dutch, the conversation died off a bit. The trick for both of them, was to find a common ground to chat about. It was the ability to speak Dutch, which had Horace ask the question.

"You are from Holland?"

"Yes, I lived there for many years." Felix was cautious.

"It's a great place to live. I especially loved the relaxed life style, and of course the fields and fields of flowers every year at spring, like, right about now." Horace, briefed in the art of questioning from his training as a detective, knew it was best to go slow.

He stopped then for awhile; his talk took a turn to the animals he was staring at. "You love your pets. What a great idea to have pets when the time is right." Horace did not say, when one is lonely or alone. He refrained from categorizing his new neighbour.

Talking about another topic was the best way to approach a new acquaintance, Horace knew, it gave them both time to feel comfortable.

Horace had no pets. He mentioned he wished he had, but his work took him in many directions, so he was not able to provide a good, stable home for either pets or marriage.

As he had hoped, revealing he was not married, gave the next turn to the man he was sitting with, hoping some information would come forth.

Felix, loyal to himself, as in years ago, gave up nothing. He was convinced, the less anyone knew of him, the safer he would be.

He knew he was right. Horace also knew he could find out if Felix was previously married, from any one of the neighbours around him, including the mother of Stacey, and Leanne.

It was not important to know if he was married, but Horace knew if he was to learn anything about his new neighbour it would be through somebody he loved. The next question would be if he had any children. Felix looked away and started to get up and follow his pets back to the house. He did it in such away, where it was not rude, just a need.

Felix did not know if this man was trying to trip him up in saying something he might regret, or if he was just being friendly. It was just too soon to talk to strangers. Even though he had lived there for quite some time, he knew the war was not far behind him and anything could happen. Also, his conversation skills were not honed, and at times he felt insecure beside others, who were well versed.

When he started walking towards the house, both Leanne and Mary - Jane were on it. Each girl took one of his arms, and walked beside him into the house.

After they came out Stacey stared at them. She was not convinced.

"You know, he doesn't look that old to me. Why is he bent over, with wispy hair and no energy?"

"Oh, Stacey, you're such a nerd. Give the man a little help, it won't kill you." Leanne was convinced Stacey was being, just that, Stacey, and of course Mary - Jane agreed with her.

It was later in the week when Horace found the answer. He had been rifling through the archives in the main library downtown, Vancouver. There were so many files, he had to be discreet, and only focus on the ones he needed to answer his questions. He came up with some amazing answers.

Chapter Fifteen

It was through the archives Horace found the answers to some of his immediate questions. He researched the Dutch arriving on the border of the United States and Canada after the second world war. He researched their disbursement, including the most populated areas.

The Dutch were skillful in business and the handling of money. Many of them had opened up stores in the downtown area for their livelihood.

The most enduring find Horace had made had to do with Felix. As a detective, Horace, was granted privilege into archives, the public would not be allowed.

Horace found out a lot about Felix. There was no need to question him on a lower-level basis, when all the answers were right there in the files.

When Felix arrived in Canada he went through customs. His name, age, heritage and background were listed.

Felix was fresh out of a concentration camp for German Jews. He was an escapee, but all the files with even a mention of him were red flagged and Horace had to pay good money to see them, even though he was a detective. Horace was shocked and at the same time, silenced by this.

Absolutely, no one in the neighbourhood had a clue about his background. Horace wondered if Mary - Jane's Mother would be allowing her to be this close to a man of this calibre. Even Stacey and Leanne may not be allowed to perform in the plays, if their Mother knew they were playing on the property of an escapee.

For this reason, Horace chose to not reveal what he learned. He knew there was no harm, and Felix was caught in a terrible situation from the war. It was not his fault and he needed protection.

Horace over the years had seen many pictures of refugees and immigrants from the war. He could not imagine going through that, and he could not imagine how much that past would haunt someone to this day.

He heard from the children, Felix slept a lot. When he did and they arrived at his front door, he was just waking up, or in a dazed state. Horace speculated he may be haunted, and may be going back in time. His studies proved this was one of the ways being held captive was dealt with, in the past. Now, there may be other ways to black out horrific war memories, but these he did not know.

"No wonder Felix was reluctant to talk," Horace felt badly now, when just a day ago, he was trying to get information out of a man who would rather not talk at all, if he had to talk about the past.

Horace kept researching records for what he himself was sent to Canada to do. He knew Felix was going to be a valuable asset for finding out the information he needed to know, for his own case.

A small elderly man sat hunched at a desk, in a corner of the library, much like a bird of prey. His tiny, oval glasses were halfway down his nose and he appeared as though he was barely breathing. On his large wooden desk, pages were scattered, but stacked in a definite order, so they weren't really scattered after all. He was focused to the point Horace thought, *"Well maybe he isn't breathing,"*

As Horace stepped quietly in front of him, there was a decided soft purring sound. The elderly man was asleep. His hair was disheveled and his brown, corduroy jacket was somewhat ragged, but still serviceable. In front of the desk was a sign which read. Humphries: Research Specialist.

Once Horace stepped up to the desk to read the plaque, the elderly man woke up. He was instantly alert. Horace introduced himself, and mentioned his need.

"Could you kindly, point me to the archives regarding the German Jews in the second world war." Horace whispered, "it is deathly quiet in this library."

The old man gave an unexpected smile. He was more than happy to extend this wealth of information. He lived for this.

"Thank-you for coming in today. Horace, you said. I want to let you know I'm here for anything you need. Follow me to the back."

Horace was more than thrilled he had found someone else who loved to be in the stacks. He could smell the old paper smell already. As he followed Mr. Humphries he had a chance to look at his clothing from the back. The man was a smart dresser, but he could see the wear on his clothing. Horace wondered, if he too was from the war years in Europe and had his own story to tell.

Once Horace reached the area he was looking for, he thanked the elderly man and started in on the shelving units that mentioned Displaced Persons from World War II.

Horace felt as though he had marched back in time. There was another sign which mentioned Pier 21.

As Horace read, he was entrenched with his new find:

Economic boom in Canada created a labour shortage, so many of them (Displaced Persons) (D.P.) were admitted as labourers.

Until 1952 almost 200,000 people were admitted under the Displaced Persons movement.

Others were sponsored but some were admitted even without secured sponsorship, travel documents, or personal I.D.

A majority of Displaced Persons were from: France, Belgium, Netherlands, Italy, Austria and Germany. They came simply, to seek better opportunities.

Horace jumped for joy in his mind. These people were from many countries, and Netherlands was one of them. He could now share this knowledge with Felix. Felix might be willing to talk about himself and his past.

Horace read on. He was fascinated by this knowledge and the stacks of information, which would be hours and hours of reading.

Mr. Humphries was back at his desk. He wasn't quite asleep yet, but he was close. Horace wondered how he was still working here when it was clear, he should be retired.

"I am only here for two hours a day." When Horace asked him about his length of time each day for further visits, he also gave him the time. Arnold Humphries, which Horace found out later, worked from 9 – 11 each morning.

"Thank-you Arnold, I will see you again soon." It was easy to ask him for his first name. He did not mind being called by his Christian name. He concluded, Mr. Humphries, was too formal.

Reaching the foyer of the library, Horace flagged down the front librarian. After mentioning Arnold, Horace realized he was kept on for his in depth, impressive knowledge on all war facts and correspondence. "He also has an incredible memory. You will find out the more time you spend with him." Gladys, the librarian had a shine in her eyes. "He is able to recite many war speeches by memory. He knows the famous speech by Winston Churchill... ".we will fight on the beaches"... by heart and he is able to say it in a voice much like Churchill himself.

Horace left the downtown library with a skip in his step. Things were looking good. He could not wait to meet up with Felix and divulge of all the information, he had gleaned today. He was hoping Felix would be more compliant and open up into a conversation.

Horace had a hint of realization Felix knew something which would help his case here in Canada. There were many men from the war who needed to be found. How Felix would know anything about this, was the hope Horace had in his heart. He had an intuition about things, this was what made him a good detective. This was how he won awards for excelling in his field. This is how he found and captured a serial killer ten years ago. Horace Hoek has numerous trophies in his office.

When Horace arrived home Helen was making lunch. He quite liked his aunt, she was always the same. Her countenance, somehow calmed and grounded him. She was always soft spoken, kind, gentle and accommodating.

Helen, he thought was more intelligent than she appeared. He could tell by watching her, she thought things through before responding. He was especially impressed with her the day she mentioned she knew Felix could speak two languages. Her example of how she knew, surprised the heck out of him. Felix was talking to Chloe and Charlie, one in Dutch and one in German. Helen had the gift of observation, and this in turn, he speculated, would be a large help to him one day.

Chapter Sixteen

Helen was watching Horace eat lunch. He was more than happy to have lunch with her. She had not talked with him alone yet, and she was looking forward to hearing more about him and his life.

She had never seen such a driven man. She knew others like him during the war, but this one she knew, was different. "He will not stop; he is on the go and on the lookout always, such a keen mind." There was something to learn here and Helen thought, she did not want to miss a thing.

Helen knew if she had a son, she would want him to be like Horace, inquisitive, intelligent, caring and compassionate. She was happy he graced her table, loved her cooking and talked to her, really talked to her.

"This man came into our lives, just when Mary - Jane needed the excitement of learning something new, such as learning the Dutch language, and learning how to play chess." Helen was thinking this in her head. She looked at his blue eyes and dark hair and saw a wonderful man, a wonderful soul.

He gave her such a grateful look and thanked her profusely for the delicious food she had offered him.

"Tell me about your childhood; I am more than interested to hear about your family and your work." Helen took off her apron, sat down, and placing her chin on her right palm leaned into him at the table.

Horace knew this would come up one day. He was totally ready. He didn't want to lie, but he didn't want to spell everything out to Helen either. His past in his mind, was hideous. The only way he could come out from under the black clouds he carried around with him, was to tell the partial truth.

Horace started in to tell Helen how he was brought up by an aunt. His father, left the family and re-married. His new family with a large number of children, took up all his time. He had no time for his first son, being Horace. Horace stayed with the aunt until he could stay no longer. His father never visited him.

Helen had tears in her eyes. She could feel the vague, desolate, lonely feeling, he must have had during his growing up years. She would never have wanted that for Mary - Jane.

Horace could see how this affected Helen, so he turned the conversation into his work and career.

"There is much to say about a family, but once the childhood stage is over, real happiness comes from pursuing a true passion. In my case it was training to be a detective. This is what saved me."

Horace could see this was a difficult concept for Helen. In her day, a woman's career was always about family, a working father to give what he could to his family, and a mother who stayed home to give her heart and soul.

Helen put the kettle on for tea. Once the tea was ready, Horace shared the teapot with her, and he kept on.

This was the best afternoon Helen had spent in a long time. She could not wait to hear more about Horace.

"My father, upon leaving gave me one thing. He gave me the confidence to try anything I wanted. I always loved problem solving, and mysteries, and one day I saw an ad." Horace stopped.

"This ad kept me up for a couple of nights. When I was nineteen I enrolled into a detective course, which to this day was my saving grace. This course was in Amsterdam, and it offered up room and board for those, who passed the numerous tests to be in the beginner program, and then the advanced program." Horace stopped again.

Helen was still listening with no questions. She kept serving tea, and her eyes became brighter and brighter when she heard what Horace trained himself to do.

"It was the brutality of the course which kept me there. There were interrogators, and for hours at a time, asked me questions I was sure nobody needed to know the outcomes. This was a test for stamina. As a detective it was imperative to: sit still for hours in a car on surveillance, ask questions to a murderer without showing favour or bias, keep on track, and look for clues with only one night to do so, before all evidence became concealed and stored away."

It was hard for Horace to not talk about the war. Most of his recent work was to do with the war. He did not want Helen, for instance, to pick up on the fact he may be looking for men who were responsible for war crimes. This would taint his visit with her, making her weary and afraid, especially with a young daughter in the house.

He was relieved when Claude arrived home, and there was a change in topic. Claude, in his own soft way declared there was something he wanted to show Horace downstairs, so off they went. Helen cleaned up the lunch dishes and the teapot tray.

Once Claude had Horace below the kitchen floor, he moved him into his work shed area so Helen upstairs, could not hear what he had to say.

What he had to say startled Horace. He was dead right about the man living behind them. Felix was an escapee and a German Jew. Claude had this to tell. He found out that day, from extensive detective work coming through a Canadian network. The only reason he did not find out the same way Horace did, was the files were sealed.

Horace was happy it was out in the open. Now, he could also talk to Claude about it openly. When Claude found out Horace knew from his research on that very same day, they opened up a bottle of scotch and clinked glasses.

"We must do anything we can, to make sure Felix is safe and not hunted. If any one comes to the door, at least now, we both know we have to hide him." Claude knew this may never be needed, but the warrants for arrests were out there, and who knew why they would arrest Felix? Being an escapee was not the same as being a guard or an officer in the Regime, hunted for war crimes.

As they poured their second drink, the next concern was for the children. So far, there were no concerns for the children. Felix was calm, kind and appreciated them very much. The only concern was they did not want the children going into his house. How they were going to stop that they did not know. They would devise a plan. Their next point would be, do they tell Helen?

It was decided they would tell Helen, but not right now. They needed time to process what they had learned. Claude and Horace knew there would be something which came out of this, but they didn't know what it was yet. They both agreed they needed a vigil - a careful vigil.

Helen wondered what was taking them so long. They had been downstairs for almost an hour and she wanted to serve dessert. When they came up, they looked weary and almost sad. When she saw Horace, he put his arm out for the plate she offered, but stopped.

"Helen, do you mind if we save this dessert for dinner tonight, Claude and I have something important which just came up?" Helen nodded with such compassion, he almost cried.

Claude went over and gave his wife a kiss on the cheek, mentioning the time they would be home.

Now, Horace knew why they decided to not tell Helen anything yet, she wore her compassion on her sleeve.

Chapter Seventeen

Felix was disappointed. When he sat down on the couch he could not concentrate. For years he had played the ukulele, but today it would not come. His love for music kept him happier than any other cell mate, so he played the notes in his head, all day long. Even now, he could play the instrument by playing the notes in his head, and not strumming anything tangible at all.

One day, he would love to be able to walk into a music store somewhere close by, and purchase a small ukulele. He dare not ask the children or adults for the location of a store, because not many people had money right after the war. Felix, knew there a would be a time when this would happen, but not yet.

As Felix stretched out on the couch, he looked at the clock. It was not time for school to be out yet, so he took a nap. His dream this time was about Horace and the house he was in. This house included Claude and Helen and

Mary - Jane. He could see Claude leaving for his work, and then there was a close up of Helen as she stretched clothes out onto the clothesline, the one with the pulleys, which squeaked.

Her close up features were familiar, and at times he found her looking at him also. This was a strange feeling, as though they both knew each other from the past.

Felix blinked in his sleep. It was though she was coming to him, and her face, was right in his face. There was a knock on the door, just then, and Felix half woke up. He was still half in his dream. He could see her face, and her face was usually quite red. She had pink in her skin, which made her look like she was outside a lot. Her nose had a little hook in it, and it was always red. She tended to blow it a lot.

After a few minutes, after rubbing his eyes, he opened the door. There she was; she was right on his property. He had never seen her up close before. In her hand she held a plate. Brimming with raspberries and topped with snow white whipping cream, she held it out to him.

"Oh, hello, I am pleased to see you." Felix stood motionless, he had no idea what to do or say to a woman. His life had been full of men for so long, he felt as though talking to a woman was a highly polished craft. He was not polished at all.

With no further passing of time, Helen reached out and put the dessert in his hand. Felix took it with shaky fingers. She smiled and left. He leaned on the door frame and tried quite hard to say thank - you, but nothing would come. His voice was kidnapped.

Helen sensed he was trying. She turned and waved. He waved back.

The dessert was so delicious, he took miniature bites and it took him a long time to eat it, purposely using one of his small forks. He was captured by the luscious sweet taste of something precious and new. Then, he thought of Heleena.

"Where was she?" He so wanted to have this woman's company. He so wanted to have a companion, a wife, and children. "When was this going to happen?" The voice talking in his head, would never stop.

The sugary sweetness of the dessert made his body relax. On the couch he stretched out and fell asleep. Now it was Heleena, who haunted his dream. There was no turning back. He relived their kiss over and over.

Banging on the door were three little monsters. Felix, called them that when they entered. They laughed.

"Why are you calling us monsters Felix, we have just come to visit?"

Leanne in her quiet voice talked him into not calling them monsters, if he could help it. He agreed, and they all laughed.

Chloe and Charlie were jumping all over them, so they all left to play outside.

Mary - Jane may I see you for a moment. They both stepped out into the sunshine. Felix did not want anyone in his house, if they could be outside.

"I have a small plate I would like you to take back to your mother. She was so kind to offer up a dessert for me today. I am extremely blessed." Felix handed her a Delft blue plate.

"This plate my mom brought from Holland. When she uses it, that means something special is being served." Mary - Jane smiled.

Felix felt special himself when he heard this. "Tell her thank-you very much."

When Mary - Jane left with the plate she went to the house right away and gave it to her mother. Helen was grateful to hear how much Felix enjoyed her sugary dessert.

Chapter Eighteen

Now that Claude and Horace were able to work together, the case they were working on could be solved faster. Claude had a case from his own detective agency and Horace had the case from Holland, he was sent over to solve, but both cases were similar.

The bottom line was both were looking for men who had found their way into Canada after the war, but were still responsible for war crimes.

At the library, Horace introduced Claude to Arnold. Arnold was so honoured to meet Claude Hoek, he practically bowed. He knew the detective work Claude had previously completed, following his work in the newspapers and on the air.

Claude was impressed with Arnold. A couple of hours a day Arnold Humphries helped people find what they needed from the historic stacks. He was more than eighty years old but never complained.

In his head, Claude wondered about the age of Arnold whom he was fast respecting. This elderly man rose in the early morning, to assist others in his field, certainly admirable.

Once Claude and Horace pulled all the books they needed from the shelves with the help of Arnold they sat for hours reading book after book with anecdotes, documents and former arrests.

Arnold knew the names of all the officers in the first and the second world war on both sides. He had memorized scripts, dialogues and as previously mentioned, speeches.

Whatever questions, Claude and Horace asked, Arnold was able to supply the answer without reference to books or the internet. He had an impeccable memory, one to be totally admired and respected. Every detail he offered up, helped put the pieces of the puzzle together. After a week of reading and researching Claude and Horace found out incredible facts not only about the war, but about an important entry point into Canada called Pier 21.

Pier 21 was the Canadian Museum of Immigration located in Halifax, Nova Scotia. This was the point of entry for one million immigrants into Canada. It was also referred to as "The Port of New Hope."

Pier 21 was an ocean liner terminal and immigration shed. It operated from 1928 – 1971; also, called the "Gateway to Canada." This terminal played an instrumental role in building of the nation. Today, one in five Canadians, have a link to Pier 21.

In World War II, Pier 21 was the point of departure for nearly 500,000 soldiers. Pier 21 is now a national historic site and museum. It is the last surviving seaport and immigration facility in Canada.

On the bottom of the page the sentence made Claude and Horace sit up and stare. "Dutch immigrants were the fifth largest ethnic group to arrive in Canada."

Felix would be one of those. He came from Amsterdam and entered into Canada. "We should ask him how he arrived on the west coast, considering he entered on the east coast. How did he have the money to travel across the whole nation?" Horace was curious.

Little did both men know Felix was extremely thrifty with his money. His quest to find Heleena kept his money hidden and out of reach. Even after he paid the captain to stow him away on the ship, and even after he offered money to Hans and his wife, Felix made sure he had funds for travel. When he arrived on the west coast he also had enough money to buy the house he now lived in at the back of Claude Hoek's property. Felix had worked for five years at the store where he met Heleena. All his money was saved as he was offered room and board at the time, having no expenses.

Claude and Horace stood up, stretched and thanked Arnold for his invaluable help once again. It was the end of the week and both men were exhausted.

Once they arrived home, Helen offered them an excellent meal coupled with a delicious dessert. After dinner there was a knock on the front door.

Standing on the front porch, was Stacey and Leanne's mom. When Claude answered the door he greeted her with immense kindness.

She had heard about Felix. After she heard about his life she was shaken. Her body language giving her away.

"He was so kind when I offered him the cinnamon buns. He asked me to sit down in his living room."

Claude invited her in. She had never been inside the house; she like Stacey, was mesmerized at how everything was so shiny and neat. She too, enjoyed the lace doilies.

Helen, with her great hospitality offered up a dessert to the girl's mother, once again served on a small, blue, Delft plate.

"He is a safe person," Claude and Horace were there to convince her of that. As soon as Mary - Jane left the living room to enter her bedroom and complete her homework, they explained.

"Felix is a German Jew, an escapee just before the war ended." Horace whispered this and Claude was nodding.

Putting down the plate, the girl's Mom put her hand over her mouth. She had no idea he was a victim of war.

Helen, who was not told yet, put her fingers to her mouth, and her eyes watered. Luckily, she hid it well, so not to bring attention to herself. She preferred to be humble.

Both men assured the women there was no danger. Felix was a middle aged man who survived the war, and they were there to protect him. Both women agreed they would not tell this recently known fact to any of the children. There was speculation already regarding other cases being announced over the air. It was as though the whole world was now in a holding pattern until war criminals were caught and sentenced.

Outside the window, Stacey and Leanne were skipping. As soon as Mary - Jane heard the knock on her bedroom door, she joined them.

All the adults stood at the largest window and watched them.

They knew they were blessed to have these children and would never want them to go through a war in their lifetime.

Horace stared wishing in his mind, one of the children skipping, belonged to him. He was middle aged already, but he never gave up hope.

He had an idea. He was going to go over and talk to Felix – just talk. Now that he knew more facts about Felix, he may ask him about his personal life. Maybe this time he will answer.

When Horace saw Felix sitting on the green bench, he saw something he had not seen yet. Felix was playing a ukulele.

Felix started to sing a Dutch folksong and Horace chimed in, recognizing it as one learned at a young age, before his father left.

"Where did you get the ukulele?"

"I had one for years, but during the war, it was confiscated."

One day last week, I found this standing up against my front door. I have no idea how it got there. I rarely use my front door so it could have been there for quite some time. The children, after school, come to the back door.

The song was still in the air. Both men found themselves humming.

"I would sure like to know who gave this gift to me, and how did they know I play the ukulele. Could you imagine if I played the piano? Would they have a piano standing up against the front door." Felix laughed at this. Horace had never seen Felix laugh. It was the most bewitching thing.

By that time all the kids and all the adults were in the back yard. Felix played the ukulele for hours. He never felt so loved, so appreciated and full of a sense of belonging. This was the best day of his life.

Chapter Nineteen

Leanne listened to Felix play the ukulele for hours. She was the one who suggested, by whispering in Stacey's ear, Felix would be perfect for their theatre nights.

"He could open the plays or close down the plays. All the neighbours on the block would love to see him, and look how happy he is playing the ukulele." Leanne had a light in her eye.

"What a brilliant idea!!" Stacey squeezed Leanne's arm and they both went into the house to organize and plan their next production.

Outside the library, the rain fell like the tears of a child. There was no end to it. Vancouver was an incredibly green city, but it was ravaged by rain, punished for its beauty.

Claude and Horace stood in front of the huge cement building, enjoying the design and the quiet of its structure. Inside the large doors, were men who protected the sanctity of its space, and men and women who respected the numerous tonnes on the shelves.

There was more to this, than they predicted. There were stacks and stacks of the written word, and countless words to be read. It was like a flowing tap, something that never ended, but until it was stopped, nothing mattered.

What needed to be stopped was the mistreatment of people and the horrors of war. When Claude and Horace opened up this story it would bring the house down. It was only fifteen years ago, men like Felix had their freedom taken away. Their story would paralyse the world.

When Claude and Horace witnessed Felix playing the ukulele like a pro they could not help but feel the sorrow, pain and hurt coming from his soul. His songs were forlorn, edgy, and sad. His eyes were closed the whole time as if wandering back to the painful days of freedom lost.

When Claude and Horace watched the faces of the children that afternoon, they too, were overcome with emotion. The children's faces haunted them as they stood outside the library. Inside the huge cement building there had to be answers; answers to stop a war from ever happening again, answers for love not hate.

Arnold was half way through his morning. He was stooped over today, more than normal. His manner exceptional, but there was something Horace noticed; his energy had diminished.

"Good Morning, Arnold!" Horace knew he loved hearing his first name. He too, was reminiscing of the first day he called him Arnold. "How are you today?

"A little bit waning, I must say." He stroked his arm as though in pain.

Claude noticed his colour was pale; he had seen many in his lifetime who had suffered from a stroke. He was hoping for none of that for Arnold.

"Follow me chaps, I have something to show you." Arnold led the way down a winding hallway towards a "Secret door." "It is called a "Secret door," but nobody ever referred to it as that because nobody knew it was here. Just a little library humour." Arnold was smiling. To make it even more humorous, there was a sign over the arc of the door that said "Secret Door." Now, Arnold was beaming.

Both Claude and Horace smiled at each other. This was the first time they had seen Arnold really smile. He had a great smile.

"I will leave you two in here. I will be leaving in an hour or so, but let me know what you find. The door is unlocked, and you will find numerous artifacts and wonderful memorabilia. The walls are full of helmets and the counters full of knives and guns, (certainly not loaded). I think you will find something in there which beckons you to come back."

As he left, both Claude and Horace found their way to the end of the dark hallway, opened the door, and turned on the light. The light at first was so dazzling, they had to shut the door. They took a step back for a minute.

Claude was under the realization, Arnold was setting them up to find a real treasure.

Once the door was reopened and the light was turned off, they could hear voices. Flickers of movement and diffused light circled the room. Up on the wall to the right was a massive movie screen. Every battle and every 'location of war' was rolling on the screen. Each battle and location, was documented in a summary, before and after the picture was shown.

The next screen showed prisoners of war being taken to a camp. All the prisoners were in striped clothing and lined up as they walked in silence, to the barracks at the back of the screen.

Not many prisoners turned to look at the camera, but some did. Three faces turned to look at the camera, and then there he was. One face was the face of Felix.

Claude and Horace stopped in their tracks. They were moving around the room looking at war time artifacts through numerous, thick, glass counter tops. A small noise took away their attention. It was the buzzing of the projector or a sound within the film, but when they looked up, they both held their breath in horror. The film moved on and they never saw the face of Felix again.

As the film moved on they lost track of the location. A new picture took up the width of the screen, screeching airplanes landing, with men in parachutes slowly dropping down.

Horace gestured toward the door and Claude followed. They walked stealthily and closed the door. There was no mistaking what they saw. Breathing in deeply, they moved down the hallway to the front of the library and found two large, fabric chairs in a corner, behind a large impressive pillar. The corner was decorated with aboriginal art.

"That was Felix!" Claude could not believe his eyes. "Here is the man we knew nothing about for many months and all of a sudden on one day we see the whole truth."

Horace was thinking out loud. "We need to know the date and place that picture was taken. Arnold is gone for the day, but we will find out tomorrow."

"Or we could ask the librarian right now. She's at the front desk, looking for something to do, I'm sure." Claude started walking over to the middle of the room and approached the desk. “Is there any chance we could see the screen again, in the “Secret Door” room? “

“You will have to wait for Mr. Humphries. He’s the specialist on all war projects. He will be back in tomorrow morning early.”

“Thank you. What was your name?” Horace, always polite, questioned her before he saw the embossed sign sitting on her desk, with her name on it.

What she pointed at was a three-dimensional sign which stated her name was Lena V. She would not give out more than what the sign stated.

Horace moved along, taking Claude by the sleeve. “Wow, she’s a nice looking woman. I will be looking for her when we come back.” Claude could not help but smile.

“Yes, you are only in your forties. I was hoping you would find someone here, someone here in Canada.”

“You want me staying with you for a longtime uncle, I can tell.”

“I have to admit, it is nice to have another male in the house. There are too many women in the house and in the neighbourhood. All I see are the friends of Mary - Jane and some of Helen’s friends, but few husbands.”

When they both returned to the house, Helen, had many questions. She was still upset about what she had learned about Felix. His past was horrific. It made her angry to think such a nice man would be treated badly. One of her questions stopped Claude and Horace in their tracks.

"Why did you not tell me what you had both learned? Why did I have to hear it only when the neighbour arrived on our door step?" Helen did not ask for much, but she felt left out.

"We just learned about Felix that morning, Helen." Claude went over to her and put his arm around her waist. "We talked about who and when we would reveal our discovery just that afternoon. We did not want the children to know so we agreed to tell nobody. The chance we took telling the girl's mother, was almost realized when the children needed to be safe from any improper stories."

Helen gave Claude a hug back. She did not stay unruffled for too long. Her faith in people was profound and it hurt her to be upset too long.

"By the way, Horace found someone at the library, he thought he might like. She is a beauty." Claude was teasing, and Horace grinned his largest grin ever.

Helen said, "Good, it was worth it then."

Chapter Twenty

Arnold did not show up the next day at the Vancouver Library. He was not seen until a week later. He had resigned, but came in to say goodbye.

The "Secret Door" was still open, so Claude and Horace were able to advance with their plans to find out where Felix was on the screen. Once the data was released, they found out he was imprisoned at a camp in Germany and had escaped across the border into Holland. He was one of only a few who managed to escape. He would not be forgotten.

Once they confirmed it was Felix, they asked for the pictures from the screen. Luckily, one of Arnold's jobs, before he retired was to have a carded copy of every shot on the screen.

Claude and Horace were able to keep a small picture of what they saw to be Felix. When they took it home to show Felix himself, Felix cried. The memory was too poignant.

Felix was so overtaken by the fact there was a picture of him on the screen, he had to see it for himself. He wanted to see the picture with the other inmates, and the area which he remembered so well, but not in a good way.

The next day, all three of them arrived at the library. The hours were longer, as it was a Friday night, especially staying open later for university students, on the weekend.

Felix followed Claude and Horace down the winding hallway to the "Secret Door." Arnold helped them find the exact day, location and picture of Felix from the coded system. Arnold came in for that reason alone; he was more than honoured to help. He knew Claude and Horace were well known detectives and he wanted to help.

When he first saw Felix in person, he practically wept. He held his hand out for a long time. No words needed to be spoken, as the depth of feeling could be felt in the whole room.

Once they had everything they needed, they wished Arnold a wonderful retirement. Claude noticed his arm was much better, and for that he was thankful.

After their good bye to Arnold, all three men reached the large entrance doors to the library. The librarian was now at her desk. Somehow, they had missed her when they arrived. Later, they found out she was shelving books.

Upon arriving at the front of the library, across from the front desk, Felix stopped in his tracks. He bent over as if ill and had to sit down. The large, fabric chairs were close, so Claude and Horace took him to that corner and sat him down. He sat up quickly, however, and turning, stared at the front desk. There she was!! There was his beloved!! The woman he had been looking for, the whole time he had been in Canada, too many years to count.

Heleena, now calling herself Lena, could sense something different in the air. There was a crackling that made her look up and pay attention. There was a noise over in the corner that she recognized. The noise was one of pain, but one of pure joy at the same time. He was calling her name: Heleena, Heleena!

She knew of no one who called her that in Canada. Nobody knew her past here. Heleena, wandered over out of curiosity. Behind the large decorated pillar in the area of the fabric chairs were three men. She recognized two of them, but did not see the third until they had moved to the side.

F – e – l – i – x !! The name dropped from her lips letter by letter, ever so slowly, like sweet syrup dripping from a tapped Maple tree. She swayed, almost fainted, and started falling to the floor. Both men reached out to catch her, but they didn't catch her, it was Felix, himself.

She kissed him with a passion she had never known, and he held her so tightly, she could not breathe. Heleena was in a confused state. It had been years since she had travelled back to Holland to see her parents and it had been years since she had seen Felix in their store. She now remembers when he first kissed her, the day three German soldiers pounded their boots into the back room where she was counting inventory.

"Is it really you?" Heleena could not believe her eyes.

"Yes, my sweet, it is me."

There is so much to tell. Claude and Horace were enraptured by this turn of events. They agreed to leave Felix there.

After taking the address of her apartment, so they knew where to find Felix, both of them gave hugs and blessings all around. They returned home. Felix was last seen holding and hugging Heleena, as though they were drowning victims.

The third floor apartment view was breathtaking, once they reached the miniature porch. The stairs were old, as though from Roman times and the atmosphere dark, like the inside of a black crayoned bottle. Felix had trouble breathing, but Heleena kept stating it was not far now. In his head, he would not have expected her to live in such a place. She looked happy and healthy, however, so who was he to judge? His head was spinning by the time he reached her tiny kitchen. Now, he knew why he liked his grass, garden and yard at home.

The kitchen was drenched in yellow. It looked as though a bouquet of daffodils was growing up one corner, and in another a wisp of white tulips showed the world, Heleena was indeed a Dutch girl from Holland. Every wall boasted a Delft plaque depicting a scene of: acres of flowers, signature windmills and Dutch people. There were pictures of people sporting the typical Dutch wide brim hat and wooden shoes. All the Delft plaques were Dutch blue and even though it was overwhelming the blue and yellow were perfect together.

Heleena did not apologize for the bright colours or for the huge display of flower art on all the walls. She was indeed an artist.

Now, they were alone together in a private apartment Felix felt shy. Heleena looked at him and could not believe her eyes. She had dreamed and waited for this moment for many months, which had unfortunately turned into many years.

Felix looked at her fingers, so scared and worried she may have a ring on he did not notice before, or worse, she would have been married. "I worried every day, every week, every month I looked for you, hoping you were not married. The suspense took a large part of my energy and after awhile I became numb to it. I knew that if that was the case, there was nothing I could do about it."

Heleena, after opening a four paned window turned around, and seeing Felix standing there, so vulnerable, sashayed up to him, pressed her finger onto his chin and gave him a large, warm kiss.

Seeing her so happy to see him, his heart pounding for joy, and his fingers wrapped around her waist, he was indeed in heaven.

When Heleena gave the tour of her small, capsule like apartment, Felix knew exactly what he was going to do. He was going to ask her to marry him and move to his house, where he had been waiting for her for what seemed like forever.

Sitting down on one of the rattan chairs, at the highly polished, round table, he accepted the hot chocolate, she placed in front of him. After sitting down across from him, they sipped in silence while they stared into each other's eyes. She, beautiful with red hair, and blue eyes, he, with dark hair, blue eyes and a partially grown beard.

He remembered her gentle ways, he remembered their first kiss, when he leaned over to kiss her again, she stood up.

Felix was an astute man. He wanted her right there, but he would wait until they were married, hopefully as early as next week.

The night was dark now, and the evening fast approaching, standing on the miniature porch, Felix could see why she was enchanted with her three story walk up; it gave her a view from high up, where she could see the panoramic view of all of Vancouver.

"I looked for you in Surrey for years." Felix was now able to un-tangle his brain, after the shock of seeing her. "I went to the immigration office every day for months and then Pier 21."

"I am so sorry, Felix, I changed my name to not be chased by thugs who beat me in our own village. They claimed my father ousted them, blaming them for stealing from him. One morning, he woke up with the doors broken into and many sacks stolen. We covered it up, so you would not go after them. We feared for your life, being a young man, thinking you could take them on. They were a group who belonged to a gang. My father would not be hurt by them, or my mother, but they went after the one person they knew my father would be hurt by the most, and that was me. That's why I had to leave. When I went home twice, I was disguised until I saw you in the shop. I could not be me, so I knew I had to leave again."

The darkness eclipsed the mood. Lights all over the city became like stars defying the universe. Felix wanted to leave with Heleena, he wanted her at his house as soon as he could, there was no way he was going to be without her again.

She drove to his house; her little car, was perfect for what she needed. The distance between Surrey, where he lived and her apartment was a little over an hour. "To think we were only this short distance away all that time." Felix felt like crying.

The rain held off until they arrived in the back yard of the most important place in his life – the house he bought when he arrived In Canada, - the place he ached out his years looking for her.

Heleena could only see what the automatic lights showed her as they blinked on. She knew the house and yard would be immaculate and as she stepped onto the grass, so far she was right.

Felix chose to go through the back door first. Here was a hall closet where numerous coloured jackets for all seasons were stored, some covered, some free, depending on the season.

Heleena could only see small corners at a time, the dimming light giving way as she walked further into the house. The persistent noise of the cuckoo clock impatiently proved it to be nine p.m. Luckily, she had brought with her night wear. She looked at the bedroom, and Felix mentioned, there were two, not to worry.

He knew she would be shy, so this first night had to be as though she was a guest. "The washroom is in there, if you would like to change."

"Yes, thank you." When Heleena entered the tiny bathroom, it was pitch black until she turned on the light. Then she saw the miraculous colour scheme. Everything was navy blue: navy blue walls, navy blue towels and face cloths, navy blue bath mats and waste bin.

She could see this was a man's bathroom; she had to grin to herself. When she looked up, a larger cursive smile grew on her lips. The ceiling was the only part of the tiny room which was not navy blue, it was a bright white. Her smile grew wider and she giggled inside. "This man is extremely unique and positively lovely."

After a good night's sleep in the guest bedroom, Heleena woke up wondering where she was. Then she knew. All she could think of was, she was a lucky girl and she was doubly pleased it was a Saturday. She could enjoy a great cup of coffee with the man she had been dreaming about since she arrived in Canada, many moons ago.

Chapter Twenty One

Breakfast was enchanting; they kept staring at each other, staring, unbelieving, they were both in the same room. Felix put his hand into the depth of Heleena's red hair cascading down her left shoulder. She put her hand on his hand. They kissed. He stood up and she stood up. They embraced; the embrace of lovers, who were only able to be lovers in their dreams.

The rapping on the door was lethal. Felix knew who that would be. The dog went wild with barking and the cat hid from sight. Strangely, enough, Heleena did not notice the cat or dog last night. She must have been in more of a trance than she realized.

Stacey, then Leanne, pushed their faces through the narrow slit in the door. Heleena was sitting. "Hello," Stacey was more than enraptured to see a beautiful woman in the house of Felix.

"May we come in Felix?" Heleena was standing now. She appeared mesmerized by the two girls. She offered them a seat on the couch.

"And who are these two beauties?" Heleena turned to Felix, she did not want to lose a moment with him. She also wanted to see his reaction to two lovely, school students, rapping on his door.

"We see Felix every day after school, and early mornings on Saturday." Leanne, exact about all things, displayed an air of efficiency.

"Well, tell me all about yourselves. I am quite keen on hearing about visiting young ladies. I would love to know your names, where you live, what grade you are in school, your best subjects....."

When Stacey spoke and then Leanne, Heleena knew these girls had been good for Felix. He was kept alive, surprised, entertained and most of all loved by the energy of these young children, and the others who belong to their theatre group. Heleena, could not wait to see their plays.

Once the girls left, there was much to do. Heleena called her real estate agent and listed her apartment. Her aunt's money had helped her buy the apartment many years ago, and now with the investment in the apartment, she and Felix could have a good life together.

Felix owned his house many years ago, so the two would be set for life. After all the finances were discussed and managed, it was time to shop for a ring and find a specialized person to marry them.

Heleena went looking for a wedding dress. After she found one, she had a great idea. She went looking for Stacey and Leanne.

In the backyard on the adjacent property Felix owned, there would be a wedding. The wedding would take place in the next week. First of all, she had to find out where Stacey and Leanne lived. She was also told Mary - Jane lived in the house in front of the property where the plays were performed.

It was a great idea, Heleena wanted all three girls to help her plan the wedding. After numerous conversations with Felix, she could tell he was enraptured by these children who supported him through some bleak times, over the past years.

All three girls were more than pleased to help. They were practically bubbling over with glee. Now that school was over for the school year, and summer was upon them, the days were long and hot and lazy.

"Where has all the time gone?" Felix was more than happy it was the end of the week. They were ready for the wedding, and all the neighbours once again sat on chairs lined up in the backyard as though it was a theatre.

Felix, could not wait to have Heleena living with him, and to call her his wife.

The colours were bright blue and the bride, ravishing. Felix could not believe his eyes when he saw Heleena walking down the manicured garden path, up to where he stood on a little hill at the end of the yard.

Prior to Heleena walking down the path, Stacey, Leanne and Mary - Jane wearing incredible blue chiffon dresses, threw white petals onto the lawn as they approached the hill where Felix was standing.

The only other people at the front were Claude and Horace. Little did they know, Arnold Humphries, their favourite elderly friend from the library was ordained to marry couples, so he was their pastor.

Once married, Felix and Heleena were invited to the house of Claude and Helen where Helen offered to cook, and cook some more, for this incredible occasion.

Once the ceremony was over, and all the neighbours arrived on the front lawn belonging to the Hoek's, the day and night was magical.

Mary - Jane was so thankful her mother was such a great cook, and that her father was so well respected, she felt honoured to be their daughter.

On the menu were many Dutch treats, a peach Flan being one of them. Mary - Jane was asked about some of the hot food, wondering what they were. She knew some of them, but the Dutch language was still new to her, so she let Horace answer all the questions. He of course, would make a lesson out of it, and she would have to pass that test like any other he put in front of her.

The evening was beautiful. Stars shone through the ink canopy, and the lights displayed by Felix, were enchanting, ethereal, and romantic. While Heleena and the girls worked on the colour scheme, and the menu before the wedding, Felix worked non - stop on the lights. The effect was magical.

Horace, Claude, and Arnold all shared in a three way toast. They agreed they had never seen a wedding toast like it, but they had fun, all stating something special they had learned about Felix, in the short time they had known him. They refrained however, from talking about his incarceration during the war. This was a special time of gladness, not a time of loneliness, or sorrow.

Hanging low under the large deciduous tree the white lights sparkled in full, emanating light to all corners of the yard. Felix, unheard by others, started to play the ukulele while others tapped their toes on the manicured grass. Everyone danced.

Felix still did not know who wedged the ukulele up outside his door, but he knew one day he would find out. Right now, it did not matter, he was having too much fun watching his neighbours dance. Heleena was dancing with the children, with Horace, with Claude and having such a great time. She had not stopped smiling all day.

Her beautiful red hair was wrapped up Dutch style with segments of a smooth braid and segments of flowing curls. The tiny braids threading throughout her hair resembled pearls at a woman's throat in the old fashioned banquet days of the eighteen hundreds.

When the darkness protruded into the light and the lights dimmed from pure exhaustion everyone went in. The wedding day would never be forgotten. Felix and Heleena stepped into their house together while all the attendees wished everyone around them a good night. The fairylike evening was over. Heleena waved good-bye to the girls and knew she would be seeing them often. She also needed to buy each of the girls a gift for helping her plan such a spectacular wedding.

Chapter Twenty Two

The next day was all business. Claude and Horace left early to be at the office early. They had a lot to research. Horace had never been to the office where Claude worked.

Claude showed Horace the file room, the presentation room, the discovery room, the evidence room and the largest of all rooms, the assembly area where detectives from out of town could sit and listen to the latest homicide facts, gleaned from each case.

When Claude introduced Horace from Holland, all the men shook his hand and welcomed him like a brother. They knew he was Claude's nephew and so with that alone, he was treated with great respect.

Horace found it interesting how they managed their meetings. They were similar to his meetings in Holland, but more refined with a little less comradeship.

Every man was dressed in a suit and tie. Horace felt underdressed, but Claude impressed upon him they were detectives and should be folded into the background. They need not be totally apparent and up front, like the well dressed politicians and police officers they were sitting with at the time.

Scott Johnson, at the front, son of a retired ex-cop and police captain was leaning against the longest table in the room, gesturing for everyone to sit. Pushing his palm out and down on his right hand he commissioned absolute quiet. First up was Horace. Horace was prepared for this and had been for a long time.

"Fellows, thank-you so much for having me today. You have probably learned from my uncle Claude, why I am here. It has been ten plus years, since the end of World War II, and although there has been progress made in tracking down criminals for crimes against humanity, there are still blockades to overcome." Horace looked around and continued. The men were sitting up and focused on his words.

Many of you know in 1946 at the Nuremburg trials there were many executions – eleven in all. These executions were carried out by the U.S. army, holding individuals accountable. Since then, more have been sentenced and others acquitted.

Horace raised his head, the clipboard he had been reading from was put onto the long table, and then he looked to the door on his left. He gestured to Claude to help him and together they brought Felix into the room.

Felix looked shy and barely smiled. He was introduced as a German Jew who was incarcerated in the second World War. When he looked up at the fifty men in the room, he smiled. All the men stood up and clapped for at least four minutes. Felix was not a crier, but he had tears in his eyes. In the door frame of the room he had just exited was Heleena. She chose to be there with him, so like she said, "he never has to go through anything alone, again."

Scott Johnson raised his arm half way off the floor again, palm down. The room was deathly quiet.

Felix talked about his imprisonment in a German jail. He talked about the endless days without much water, or food. He talked about the men thrown into the prison cell with him. Many of them had died from exposure, starvation, or when taken out of the cell for punishment, they never returned.

No questions were asked. It was as though the men in the room, were frozen. Heleena chose to stay inside the door frame, far enough in, so the men in the room could not see her. She was stationed there on a chair, but she could see Felix.

"We have new evidence there was a list obtained from the cell where Felix was imprisoned. He is here to attest to that." Scott Johnson, man of a few words, was willing to help Felix out to start.

"I will now turn the floor back over to Felix."

"Thank-you Captain Johnson." Heleena could see Felix was becoming more comfortable, the longer he spoke. She was proud of him for being forthright but not bringing attention to himself. He remained humble at all times.

"I will set the scene for what I noticed and had discovered at the time. As I mentioned, many men were thrown into my cell, some survived, most did not. When it slowed down, it became quieter than usual, it was then, I could hear two men whispering at the front of my cell. They were younger men than I, this was ten years ago, and I was barely twenty."

"These men were ambitious, all they wanted to do was topple the Regime. Their whispers, I could hear every night, past the hour all the cells were full, and the guards were changing shifts. It appeared as though on a rough cement table outside my cell door, they were looking closely at a piece of paper. When I was privileged to see it from a standoff view point, I saw it was a list of names." Felix continued.

"Every night I positioned myself in the cell to hopefully catch a glimpse of the names and commit it to memory. So many times I came close, but the men were mean and would bang on the cell bars to stop me from peeking over. I resented their cruelness and knew one day I would succeed." The room was quiet, much quieter than before. All the men were listening as though they were in his story. Felix kept looking over at Heleena; she too was mesmerized.

"After many months, many moons, and very few suns I saw a way which could be of help. It appeared every time a prisoner block had to be moved or new prisoners placed, the cement table in the front of my cell was vacated. There were no guards there."

"I moved closer to the cell bars to hopefully find names that I thought would be helpful to me if I escaped, or if I knew these names for future reference, to make a deal. In actuality, I probably had no idea why I needed these names, but something kept pressing me on." Felix was offered some water, then he continued.

"One night, like many others, the guards were called to help move prisoners, and to bring in new ones. The whistle, this time seemed more urgent, catching the two guards outside my cell off guard (so to speak). They were startled and ran out as if they were being hunted. When I looked at the table where they usually read the list of names, the list remained on the table. One must know, however, only a few minutes before the whistle, I had asked one guard for a glass of water. He practically snarled at me, but offered up a glass (actually a tin cup) of water. When the whistle blew, the guard was so startled he neglected to close the cell door securely and it swayed open a bit on its hinges." Felix smiled ever so slightly, on the next part of his talk.

"With the door on its hinges, slightly swaying and the list on the table, I saw an opportunity; I found my way to escape. Luckily, the man who had just been thrown into my cell was fast asleep."

The fifty men in the room, once slouching, all sat up and now they were more alert than ever. Felix continued.

"Ever so slowly, I opened the cell door wider. At times it would squeak, so I was prepared for this. I took the list off the table, rolled it up and stuck it inside my underwear, (which wasn't too clean by the way)." The men laughed, not only because it was funny, but to ease the rising tension.

Felix continued, almost in a monotone. He could see Heleena with her palm over her mouth, in disbelief.

"I tiptoed to the entrance and saw no one. All the soldiers and guards were now standing on a large hill, which I knew to be the marshalling area. They all had their backs to me. I saw the forest to my right and walked to it, like I was a visitor in a capital city. To this day, I don't know how they didn't notice me. The noise at the front where they were staring, had them hypnotized.

I walked into the forest, making sure I did not step on dry twigs. I knew the last escapee was caught from that small noise. I walked on the padded earth where no sound emulated. I walked for days.

Scott looked at Felix and suggested they take a break. He was glad to do this, as this first part of his talk was completed. The next part would narrate his journey from escaping Germany, through Holland and his travels to Canada as a stow away.

Felix went immediately over to Heleena. She had never heard his life as an inmate. She hugged him hard and he hugged back. They were in each other's embrace when Scott offered them a seat at a lovely round table with a white table cloth. The food spread on the longer table, also with a white table cloth, was equal to a dinner buffet.

Most of the men ate in silence. There was a definite calm over the room where it was almost sacrilege to talk or make any noise.

Felix felt totally respected in this environment. He was convinced his words had an effect, on his audience. Once again, he felt humbled and not uplifted to hero status. He knew the whole point of the talk was to give the knowledge of the most horrific event of his life.

The lunch was celebrated by all, many thanks went up to the cooks and the organizers. Some of the men were honoured to give a small token in a tip jar.

When all fifty men found their seats, and the room went quiet, only then did Scott go to the front. He compelled the men to listen to the next journey where Felix, on his own as an escapee, was now trying to get out of Germany. "This was a dangerous game. I now invite Felix back up to give us the rest of his harrowing journey."

The applause was loud. Once Felix was stationed at the front, once again, all the men stood up and clapped. There was so much love and respect in the room, Heleena, fine in her own corner of the door way where she could see Felix, started to cry.

"When I say, I walked into the forest like I was visiting a capital city, I meant it. I did not run, I did not flinch, I did not hide, I just took a stroll. The men on the hill were not looking my way and I was actually fearless. Now, when I think about it, I shake."

Some of the men giggled a little, but most seemed as though they were thinking all the same thing - how would they have felt?

Felix continued. "As I walked through the forest, I realized one thing; I knew mapping. I had studied maps as a kid, as an adult, as an inmate. There was no doubt in my mind the border to Holland was near. All the maps deliberated the slope of the land, the foliage and the proximity of Germany to the Netherlands. I could tell by the landscape and the smoke coming out of the chimneys of cottages, I was close. There was also a windmill in the distance.

I followed the smoke trail and found a cottage. The next best thing, which I remembered, seeing in movies, was a clothesline. This was the most memorable to me. Out of all the things I needed most, was a change of clothes, out of prison stripes.

After grabbing what I needed off the line, I narrowly escaped a woman coming out waving a rolling pin. If she got me, I would have been rolled to death, (the men laughed). Finding a large root to bury my stripes I put on the clothing from the line, and was surprised they fit. I had probably lost twenty pounds, so of course, knowing this, I had inadvertently, grabbed the smallest size.

The next few days were harrowing. I climbed to the top of the highest cliff and looked down. There was a lot of commotion and I could hear more whistles. They were on to me, I had to be careful. I knew the border was close so I maintained a low profile. Up in the rockiest area I had found a cave and slept for two nights. When the noise below became louder, I had to leave the cave and find a better place where I would not be cornered. The area I chose was a low hole in the ground like a ditch, behind numerous deciduous trees, off the beaten trail. In my mind, I wondered if there was a dog tracking team after me, but for some reason I could not hear any dogs. I think

I was just lucky. They thought I was much closer and the dogs may not have been needed." Felix stopped to breathe more deeply and to process the words he had just spoken, for himself and the men in attendance.

"It was the next day, when all the noise below the cliff had subsided I looked to a bridge I had noticed. It was now teeming with people. This was a direct bridge into Holland. It looked as though there were no guards checking for papers and that remains a mystery to me today.

I now took a chance. I had to get into another country. I walked the bridge with nothing in my arms and so I must have looked like a local, who at this time of day was either going to work or coming home. I was wearing clothing which looked like work pants and a shirt. The only item missing was a construction hat. As it was, I walked free and my heart soared. I was now in Holland.

Starving for days, I looked for the closest shop where food was apparent, outside in the bins, inside on the shelves. I looked tattered and it was post war, so Hans, the store owner took pity on me.

"Son, you're looking a little gaunt, if I must say so myself. Let me offer you, whatever it is you desire to eat just for this day."

"I was so taken aback I offered to work for free for room and board. Hans offered me croissants and cheese and in the end milk. Once the day was over and all the work was done, I was offered more food, and then I was able to look at my lodgings. Hans and his wife had a lovely home above the shop. In their store they sold grain in sacks, and numerous flowering plants. They also had a small bakery, and knew of a fellow farmer who had a dairy.

I stayed with Hans and his wife for a long time. I have failed to mention, so far, Hans and his wife had a lovely daughter named Heleena. (At that all the men snickered as they knew the woman in the back room was exactly her - Heleena).

I must tell you how I learned about Heleena. It was the beginning of my plight. Only a couple of days after the croissants and cheese, did the German soldiers find their way into the village. I was helping Hans at the front of the store when Hans himself, knew the German soldiers may have been looking for me. He told me in a very calm voice to go to the back room and count inventory.

Once I was back there, through the knothole in the door I could hear three German soldiers come in and ask Hans questions about an escaped Jew they were hunting down. Luckily, Hans was not lying, because he did not know I was an escaped Jew. If he was lying the German soldiers would have been able to tell. They were experts in this field. If someone was lying to them, the consequences were brutal. Once I heard the pound of their boots in the store, I had to enact a plan, and fast. I could see Heleena in the corner counting inventory. I could hear the boots coming closer to the door of the back room.

Stepping lightly over to where Heleena was standing, I gently covered her mouth with my hand. She squirmed a little, but stopped when I told her there were Germans coming through the door, to the back room, where they were. Her eyes grew big. When I kiss you, pretend we are lovers back here, our heads will be turned so they cannot see our faces. Do you understand?

Heleena shook her head, in that same moment the Germans came bursting into the room. I kissed Heleena like she had never been kissed before, (I was hoping). The men snickered again.

"Once the Germans saw we were not going to stop, they said something about young lovers and left. They are not big believers of open courtship." Felix stopped. He felt exhausted.

Chapter Twenty Three

After the break, Felix continued. The men were entranced by this story; they were not only entranced, they could not believe it. If they read it in a book, it was just a story, but it really happened and it happened to this fine young man standing right in front of them. Scott Johnson relayed this to the group, just before they all sat down, one more time.

Heleena, was feeling sleepy. She noticed Felix was flagging and hoped his story was almost completed. In her head she was thinking, maybe, they should have made two days of this talk; the emotion of it was draining Felix.

As it turned out, Felix completed the story in the next half hour and they were able to wrap themselves into each other's arms and go home.

However, before that happened here is what Felix shared.

"In Holland, I worked for Hans and his wife for many years. Heleena, had travelled to Canada, and I did not know where. Her father was not sure, but her mother knew Heleena was staying with her sister.

When I could not find her, I needed to journey to Canada to find out why she left Holland and only returned twice.

I saved all my money, and when I left I gave a large portion to Hans and his wife, and the rest to a ship Captain to stow me on board.

I spent many days down at the wharf, looking for a ship and a Captain who would do this. Stowing a passenger on board was a serious offense. The Captain could have been arrested and his ship besieged. The Captain, I hired, however, was in desperate need, so he agreed to take my money and we sailed the next day.

I landed in the port of Vancouver, British Columbia, Canada and looked for Heleena for five years. She was known to be living with her aunt in Surrey, a small rural area outside of Vancouver. I thought she must have married, because with all the visits to immigration and Pier 21, they had no record of her name.

Then I met Claude through Horace, who arrived from Holland. He arrived on the doorstep of Claude and Helen Hoek. Horace was a nephew on Claude's side. Both men had won awards as detectives of the highest order in their own country. Researching their own cases took them to the war room in the Vancouver library, and that is where the next story begins.

Heleena and Felix stopped and approached Scott together. They asked if they could complete the rest of the story the next day. Scott was disappointed. He wanted the men who were already there to hear it all.

Felix and Heleena were grateful for this chance to tell their story, but Felix had not been up in front of that many people ever, and he was winding down.

"The only reason I cannot stop is all the men are only here for the rest of the day. They go home in different directions after this presentation. It cost the city a substantial amount of money to have them here. What if we as a group adjourn the meeting and re - convene about 6:30, after dinner.

Both Heleena and Felix agreed. They went home to have a nice dinner and to relax.

When the time arrived Felix found himself at the front of the room again, to continue his story. This was the part of the story he was worried about. Heleena, Claude, and Horace, none of them, knew the rest. Felix looked around at the crowd. He was about to tell the part of the story, only he knew. He was about to extend himself into the realms of mystery, where there would be no turning back.

He may be in a dangerous position if he was charged with holding back information. This was the late 1950's and many executions were already carried out. He had a list of men who were in the Third Reich, but had never produced this information. He could be held in contempt and jailed.

The war was over, and he had done nothing wrong. The only thing Felix did was hide a list of names. He had to remember that was all he did. He had not hurt anyone, killed anyone or left anyone behind. Once he started his story, the completion of his total journey, he would be done. He also wanted to make sure his list matched the list of the men from the Nuremberg trials. What if there was one man on his list they were looking for and he had the information?

This last possibility careened him forward. He was now ready to divulge in the last part of his past.

"As you all know from my first two presentations, I was imprisoned for some time before I escaped. When I escaped I was fortunate enough to find my way into Holland. There, I was free. However, before that, I was not. I was still in Germany, but I had a secret. I had hidden a document inside my underwear as I walked out of the prison. This document was found outside my jail cell, on a cement table. The guards pouring over that list were suddenly taken away for an urgent prisoner exchange. When they left, I noticed my cell door ajar, only slightly, but I pushed it open and walked out. I walked through the forest, but my major concern was finding a hiding place. I had to find a place for the document.

I certainly, could not be caught carrying it around, so I had to keep my wits about me. When I found a place to hide it, I had numerous scares about who might find it. It was a list of all the officers of the Third Reich who had been in charge of numerous crimes in the camps. There were twelve names in all. I found one spot, then another, then another. The last location was up north in an area which had become overgrown and uninhabited. I could tell this place was not lived in or occupied.

The place, once a log cabin, was now a shack. It bore no resemblance to a place anyone would be living in. The logs on the cabin walls and the dilapidated roof were attest to that. I knew nobody would be returning, to live or sleep there.

I spent time piling up the bracken ferns around the area, and at night, I slept there. It was amazing how soft a bracken fern bed is when one is dead tired. Food was scarce, but I snared rabbits and ate berries. I was careful to exist behind the shack when cooking and to disable the smoke. I wanted no visitors." Felix had all the men sitting upright in their chairs. The moment of truth was upon them and they could feel it.

Finally, deciding on the area and the shack where my document would be hidden I looked around all sides. The back was a good idea, but, it was not settling in my brain, to be right. The area must not be obvious, if anyone were to stumble upon the shack and be nosing around. The sides and front were no better. I sat one night looking at the fireplace and wondered ... there were brick inside which were never disturbed.

However, the minute I disturbed one, it practically crumbled under my touch. The bricks were fragile. I thought what about a brick further in, not used, not fragile, but still able to hide a thin page of paper.

That was it. I took the second from the front brick out, and sure enough it was able to stand a thin crust of paper. I put the second brick back in and then the first. The first brick could be seen from the front of the fireplace, which was fine, but the second brick was hidden totally. Who was going to come there anyway?

I know exactly where the list is. I have co-ordinates to find the shack, and the list should still be intact. Now, I need a team of men to climb with me and find this location. We will all find the list together and match the list from my prison cell to the list of the U.S. army. If the list of the U.S. army is short one person, as they appear to be, it will be on the list I have hidden. I know that for sure.

In this way, we will have all the men accounted for, who thought they could get away with crimes against peace and humanity."

Felix stopped. He turned to his left to see Heleena smiling. All the men stood up again, and clapped as though Felix had done a monologue in a theatre.

There were takers, takers who volunteered to help bring the list home. Men who wanted to be a part of the mission, to end the evil of war, to make men accountable.

Scott set up a sheet for the men to sign in. They were able to sign up six to eight good men to take the journey and follow Felix, Horace, and Claude into the Dutch wilderness. They would find the log cabin, and hope the list is still between the bricks, where Felix indicated he had hidden it from view.

The date was set, two weeks from now, they would all head out. There was much planning to do before that.

Chapter Twenty Four

Felix spent numerous days and nights listing the supplies needed for nine men to take the trek to the hidden log cabin in the woods. Needed, were the supplies for travelling, food, bedding and some weapons.

This was still a time of post war, so they needed to be extra careful. Their long journey would take them over the landscapes of Germany and Holland.

First of all, they needed to fly from Vancouver to get there and find lodgings. Hans neighbours and friends, were notified, who then offered their homes to the nine men. This was a lot to ask, but they were more than excited to hear about what Felix, Claude and Horace were willing to do, to track down the list of men who were being hunted for crimes against humanity.

Horace had a house in the south of Holland, but it was too far to use for this mission. They were pleased Hans and his neighbours were closer. Even though Hans was no longer there, he had relatives who were living in his house and there was room for all three men. The other six who had signed up were delegated to the neighbours.

Felix, after all his planning realized he had one problem; he could plan all he wanted, but he could not take all the supplies on the plane. His next written letters were to the neighbours in Holland, who offered up their homes for lodging. His further request was: were they able to offer up back packs and bedding? Felix, Claude and Horace would pay them handsomely for the food.

The food was able to be cooked like camping food, with little work and in most cases just water added. They would be using camp fires along the way, and small tents for coverage against exposure. The summer months were almost over, it could be cooler any time now, especially in the higher areas.

There was one week left. Felix decided to have a meeting with the men who had signed up. They all agreed to meet at the house of Felix. It seemed few people had seen his house, which Stacey and Leanne called a museum. It was filled with whittled statues, animal pictures and war artifacts.

When the men arrived, Felix along with Claude and Horace made them comfortable offering up drinks and food prepared by Helen. Helen was so excited to cook for this adventure she had a huge buffet waiting for them.

Once the men settled in, they looked at the large list on the wall which Felix had resurrected. There were lists of supplies, food, bedding, and small weapons. All nine men read the list for what they deemed to be needed. Everything was listed, Felix had done a commendable job.

The only problem they were having is the expense of it all. The plane ticket, the transportation from the airport to the site, the cost of food and the trek. Felix had expanded his research to find out ways to cover the cost. He decided to go to the U.S. army and ask for travel funds.

He was in luck. The army, more than happy to help, offered up all nine plane tickets to be paid and a stipend for food and lodgings.

Once the men heard this, they were more than relieved. Their journey took on a new lustre, free from debt.

The six men who volunteered had families. They were pleased to hear they would be looked after. All they needed to do was give their time.

In the next few days, they would all be driven to the airport and fly out. Felix wanted to see one more play before Stacey and Leanne and their troupe folded up for the fall.

They chose a comical one to lift the spirits of the men who were leaving. All six men and their families were given front row seats to watch Pinocchio, a chosen play for the smallest children in the families.

Felix, being the good sport he was, chose to be Pinocchio. He said, he was the true choice, because he had a longer nose. All the kids laughed and laughed. The actors did a wonderful job, and everyone left in a great mood. Heleena, hugged Felix until he couldn't breathe.

The next day the group left for the airport. The flight was long, but at the end of it, all the men landed in Holland. They were then picked up by the neighbours who offered them lodgings.

One day of rest was next and then the trek would begin.

Felix had maps and a compass. His theory was the same. If he followed the path he knew, he would see the cabin in the distance by the third day.

All the men trusted Felix, and he was slowly becoming a hero to them. His appetite to find the last man and make him accountable was admiral. Two days after they landed, a briefing with all the men and the packing completed, their time at their lodgings came to a close. There was no more to say; the next step was climbing the never ending terrain which would take them to greater heights.

The camping food was surprisingly delicious, even though all they had to do was add water, cooking it to a prescribed heating point over an open fire. The days were still sunny and bright, being September, but in the higher elevations, the nights were cooler. The hot meal at the end of the day was as Claude was quick to say, "Absolutely wonderful, but not as good as Helen's." All the men agreed. They took turns slapping Claude on the back.

Each man had a wool army blanket, wool clothing and thermal underwear. Their boots were tall, knobbed and a high end brand.

Luckily, one of the six men was a registered first aid man, so he was in charge of watching the men for fatigue, dehydration, and foot sores. His name was Ted, and he had a deep foreign accent. Nobody knew where he was from, he was quiet, and shy. Back at home he was one of the best policemen the department had.

The days grew weary and slow. The bracken fern on the ground was slippery when it rained, so as they traversed uphill they all took care to watch each other. They were tied with a strong rope at the end, especially where the cliffs became rigorous and rough.

The next night they shared their stories. Many of the policemen from Surrey and the Vancouver area agreed to come on the trek due to the fact they had a father, a grandfather, or an uncle affected by the horrors of war. Some of the stories were horrific and in the end, some of the men turned in early to eradicate themselves from memories or the stories from their families.

The small tents set up, each enclosed three men at a time, and on the last night the storm was so bad, they almost lost all three. The tall coniferous trees dripped rainwater on the tops of the tents, but it was still dryer and warmer to stay in the tent than head out.

Once they reached the infamous Vaalserberg, the highest peak In Holland, Felix knew they were getting close.

One morning the sun was so bright, they all had sun burns by midday. All men wore thick sun glasses, but it was their faces not their eyes Ted was worried about. He had cream for everyone and literally saved them. Claude went over and slapped his back, giving him the nod of appreciation they all felt.

Once they arrived at the base of the highest peak, Felix stopped and told the men his plan. His plan was to travel around the base of the peak and find himself once again in a low lying flat part of the country. He then described the shack for all the men to find. He was becoming more excited by the minute. He knew this last stand, would be the one he had been waiting for, for a long time.

"We will traverse a small part of the circumference of Vaalserberg and then find ourselves on a plain that reaches the horizon." Felix gave the men his coordinates, so they would not be lost from the group.

The rest of the journey was quiet. Arriving on the other side of the peaked mountain became the best part of the journey. The large spread out plain, Felix had mentioned, sprang into view. There was no denying it, the horizon was beautiful, and golden, inviting them to be there.

Once all the men arrived into what they termed to be the marshalling area, they took off their back packs. Sitting down with legs stretched out, the ones who smoked took out their packages.

"There is nothing better than a smoke on a clear day, after a rigorous workout." Horace, quiet on the trek, now became animated.

"You're so right, mate." Everyone laughed as Mel, the Aussi in the group gave his opinion first hand. Mel, as good as Ted in the police force had arrived from Australia with his family two years ago.

"This is where we rest mates." Everyone smiled at that. Felix was talking now, more excited than ever. They had finally arrived.

The men put up their tents while there was still daylight. Chuck started the fire. "This is our last night of dining out, or is it in." He had everyone laughing.

The food that night was almost a steak. They had all agreed they would keep the contents of the can which apparently tasted most like steak, until the end. The idea was perfect. The taste of steak was real.

Chapter Twenty Five

The next day it poured rain. September rain was warm and comfortable, but their slickers were wet and glistening. Each man slung a back pack around his shoulders, wiggled from right to left to balance the back pack and then formed a line.

Forming the line they checked each other for supplies, and a secure pack. The most important part of each pack was the thermos containing water. During the time of his escape Felix found where the waterfalls were located. They were small, trickling down the side of cliffs, but enough for the men to have a continual supply of fresh water every day.

Felix was at the front of the line in command of the compass and coordinates. He moved quickly and stealthily, each man duplicating his long strides.

After one half hour of hiking, the sun projected itself onto the tall golden grass. The rain stopped.

This was the third day and Felix knew it was the one where they would all see the cabin on the horizon. "What if I am wrong?" he condemned himself just a little. "It would all be for nothing," he looked up.

He knew he was right, however, but the way seemed a lot longer than he remembered. Then he saw it. He saw the cave where he had hidden and slept for two nights. After the noise of the guards, and after he moved again, that was when he saw the cabin.

First, he had fled to a ditch among the coniferous trees; he realized hiding in the cave gave him no way out.

It was after he moved away from the cave when he saw the cabin up on the hill; the sun projecting through its tattered shell. He was excited.

Felix stopped. All the men stopped as well. If anyone was watching it looked like a line of dominoes, they almost tripped over each other.

"There it is!" Felix almost ran to what was left of the cabin. He could not believe the shack was still standing. The wood was now no longer a painted brown, it was white and brown, roughly striped. The elements had done their damage, rain, snow and sun.

In his mind Felix was not daunted. He knew as long as the fireplace was still intact, that was all they needed. He put his back pack down on the ground. The men did the same; they were heavy after the long trek, and a relief to have off their shoulders.

Felix ran towards the broken lumber of the cabin. All the pieces, after the many years Felix had been away, had become almost decomposed. He looked around. As he predicted there was no signs of life and no signs of anyone having been there. He took a step inside.

He stopped in his tracks. The fireplace was intact, erect displaying the undisturbed red bricks. The men stared at it. Felix wondered what they were thinking.

"So, this is the real deal, the reason we have been eating out of cans and not real steak, eh mate?" Mel, true to form made the men laugh again.

"I believe so," Felix responded. "However, just think, if what I know is buried alongside the brick in that fireplace, I know we will have evidence for mankind, to hold another individual accountable for crimes against humanity. I will take that over a real steak any day." All the men clapped.

"Mel, would you like to do the honours?"

"What's that mate?"

"I would like you to pull out the second brick. I will pull out the first one, because I know how it crumbles." Felix was ready.

"Absolutely." Mel was also ready.

Felix pulled out the first brick, and it crumbled in his hand just as he predicted.

Mel, with a little hesitancy pulled out the second brick and had it positioned in his palm. On the underside was a piece of paper. Felix was concerned the list 'writing' would be damaged or faded over the years. He was more than happy to see it had not. He knew the guards had used an instrument much like a durable pencil. The list had not changed.

All the men crowded around to see the list of twelve men whose German names were distinctly written. Felix knew there were eleven men executed at the Nuremberg trials but this list had one more. Once the names were checked against the U.S. army list it would be easy to see which name stands out.

Once the army knew which man to search for and hunt down, all the worst offenders for crimes against humanity would be found.

Before the mission, Felix gave strict instructions about finding the list. "When, we secure the list, I do not want anyone including myself to read the names out loud. This gives the names power, and even though that sounds superstitious it still holds some merit. So, the names will not be read out loud." Felix was adamant.

All the men knew what Felix wanted and respected his wishes totally. This was a day for celebration.

Chuck, the cook, had a surprise for all of them. He had kept back a liter of whiskey which he offered up to all the men, to take a swig. This kept them warm and gave them a time to reminisce and a time to celebrate.

Once darkness nestled in they all sat around the remains of the inside of the cabin. On this night, no tents were erected. The sun blared through the rough timber, and the rain held off.

The mission was completed. The men moved quickly to backpack their way through the country side. They stayed one more night using the hospitality of Hans' old neighbours.

Once the celebrations were completed and the supplies returned, Felix and his men caught their flights home, the next day.

The list was well received. Helen and Heleena both stared at it for a long time. They could see why Felix did not want the names read aloud. There was a haunting there, right on the page, in between each German name. Helen, did not want to look at it any more.

Once the list was hidden away for the night, Felix made it his mission the next day to seek out the General of the U.S. army and disclose his findings.

When Felix arrived at the army headquarters he had the document between two flat pieces of glass and then wrapped in a specified cloth. There was no way it was going to be damaged at this late date.

General Closs was enamoured. He could not tell Felix how much he appreciated his work. There was going to be an awards night to distinguish his find.

Felix did not care about an awards night. He was just happy to find the one last person to be hunted down for war crimes. In a couple of days the two lists would be shared and examined. Once the name on the list Felix brought forward was established, the hunt for the last person, would begin.

Already, the U.S. department for war crimes had an idea as to where the last person discovered on the list, was now living. They were certain he was still alive. If he was not, they knew the name of the last person, who was accountable for war crimes.

This to Felix was a piece of history. This history would be written in all the new history books. Students in high school would not only study these names, but know how important history is for the sake of keeping others accountable and fighting crimes against humanity.

Many students would write reams of paper on it, write their thesis on this and know how important their democracy is after many years of war.

Felix would go into the classroom and talk about his incarceration. Students would be visiting, on large school trips the sites where imprisoned people and races were held and then killed; their freedom lost forever.

Students would know the meaning of life with freedom. Life with the firm belief, they would be able to be who they want to be. They would understand the importance of a government: of the people, by the people and for the people. Their lives would be to fight for Democracy, at all costs, to win, and never let it go.

Chapter Twenty Six

The celebration of what Felix had found and the safe return of the nine members on the mission, would start tomorrow. Felix was feeling upbeat and happy. He held Heleena in his arms. How he had waited for her for so many years; how the years had passed before he could bring home the 'list'. It had all finally come true. Felix could not be happier with this segment of his life.

Heleena was drafting up a list of food she wanted to make for the buffet. Stacey, Leanne, and Mary - Jane were the runners between houses; offering up lists of food which their mom's could make. Any specialties were noted, and offered to whomever made it best.

They were sent on wild goose chases to the attics or basements to find large mixing bowls, casserole dishes, and three tier stainless steel trays for desserts, such as brownies, dream squares and matrimonial cake.

The girls were taught how to iron tablecloths and were shown how to put them on the tables. There was no room for a crooked tablecloth.

All this to serve the many people from the neighbourhood, including the six policemen and their families. Felix, also invited many men and recruits from the army including General Closs and his family.

The backyard was looking beautiful, the lawns immaculate and now some of the taller men were stringing up lights, crisscrossing the yard creating a design, which looked like a web, from an aerial view. The theme was magical.

Tables were set up for hot food, cold food and dessert. There was no end to what food item was offered.

Helen completed her buffet list with Dutch food, a neighbour down the street offered up Hungarian food and Stacey and Leanne's mom made her specialized English Yorkshire Pudding.

Stacey, later in the week commented. "I still don't know how mom kept the Yorkshire Pudding hot for that many people. She also made a perfectly thickened, brown gravy." Stacey licked her lips telling this story.

"Even dad, who cares little about gatherings, especially with large crowds, could not walk away from the food table. He was seen lingering over the Yorkshire Pudding. After that was finished, he lingered longer over the three tier, dessert trays on the dessert table. He loved Mom's brownies, dream squares (with coconut and cherries) and matrimonial cake. He called matrimonial cake, maternity cake and to this day every one cannot stop laughing at his comical comments." Leanne was grinning as she reminisced about her father, putting her arm through his bent elbow.

Claude was back on track. Over the trek, he was quiet. He let Felix be the leader, and he watched him every minute. Mary - Jane shadowed her father the whole night. She could not help but tell her dad how proud she was of his detective work, how she loved and admired her uncle Horace and how Felix had become a friend of the family.

Little did Felix know, it was Claude and Mary Jane who bought him the ukulele, leaning it up against an outside door. Somehow, Leanne remembered him talking about the fact that he played. This was going to be the surprise of the night.

Claude clapped and then he tinkled a glass for quiet. He was going to make a speech and then a toast.

"Thank-you to all the people who gathered here tonight. I want to thank all the men who took time out of their lives to complete a mission, and a trek, to solve a very important part of our history. As a group of men, we salute you in carrying out a mission lead by our gallant Felix here," Felix took a whimsical bow.

"If it wasn't for Felix and his steadfastness to bring back the list, we would not be moving forward, never solving the last piece of the puzzle, or closing up the war crimes file, for good.

I would like to thank General Closs, who I cannot believe, is standing in my backyard, as though he has nothing else to do (many laughed at this). I would like to thank the men and recruits who have honoured us with their presence this afternoon." Claude picked up a glass of white wine.

"I would now, like to make a toast to all the men, but let us not forget the initial start of this fabulous mission. Where did it start?"

Most people standing on the lawn did not understand this question so Claude dove in. "The initial start of this mission came from the three young ladies, standing before us. These three young ladies I speak of are: Stacey, Leanne, and Mary - Jane. What did they do?

Over the past summer and current school year, these three young ladies befriended a neighbour right in our backyard whom nobody knew." Claude walked over to where the three girls were standing and with his arm around the backs of them, pulled them into his realm.